THE SAINT
SEES IT THROUGH

by

Leslie Charteris

In which the Saint finds dope
and crime in Cookie's Cellar...
and a dangerous charmer.

published by

Hodder and Stoughton
ST. PAUL'S HOUSE · LONDON E C 4

LESLIE CHARTERIS

THE SAINT BOOKS

These are the titles in order of sequence
(the original titles are shown in brackets)

THE SAINT
SEES IT THROUGH

Leslie
Charteris

The villains in this book are entirely imaginary
and have no relation to any living person

FIRST PUBLISHED AUGUST 1947
SECOND IMPRESSION JULY 1950
THIS EDITION (RESET)   1951

Made and Printed in Great Britain for
Hodder & Stoughton Ltd., London, by
Hazell, Watson and Viney, Ltd.,
Aylesbury and London

CONTENTS

CHAPTER ONE

How Simon Templar spent a Night Out, and Avalon Dexter took Him Home

SIMON TEMPLAR lighted another cigarette, took a sip of his latest and most anæmic-looking highball, and reflected with considerable gloom that if the vanquishing of villains required any man like himself to endure certain unpleasantnesses and discomforts, there must be a lot of more attractive and entertaining places to endure them in than a joint with a name like Cookie's Cellar, situated in a rejuvenated basement in the East Fifties of New York City, U.S.A.

Such, for instance, as any reasonably busy boiler factory in any moderately insalubrious zone of reconversion.

For instance, in the boiler factory he would not have been offered Little Neck clams to whet his appetite. But then, after succumbing to the temptation, he would not have been faced with a soup plate full of water enlivened with a few fragments of weary ice among which floated, half-submerged, four immature bi-valves which had long ago decided that the struggle for existence was not worth it. In the boiler factory, he would not have been able to order a rare *filet mignon*; but then, he would probably have had a real appreciation of the lunch in his plastic pail.

In the boiler factory there might have been a continual cacophony of loud and nerve-racking noises; but it was very doubtful whether they could have achieved such pinnacles of excruciating ingenuity as were being scaled by the five frenetic sons of *rhythm* who were blowing and thumping their boogie-woogie beat on the orchestra dais. There might have been smoke and stench in the air; but they would have been relatively crisp and fresh compared with the peculiarly flat sickly staleness of the vaporised distillate of cigars, perfume, and sweat that flowed through the happy lungs of Cookie's clientele.

There might have been plenty of undecorative and even vicious men to look at; but they would not have been undecorative and vicious in the sleek snide soft way of the chair-polishing champions who had discovered that only suckers work. There might have been a notable dearth of beautiful women who wore too little, drank too much, and chattered too shrilly; and it would have been a damn good thing.

But Simon Templar, who was known as the Saint in sundry interesting records, sat there with the patience of a much more conventional sanctity, seeming completely untouched by the idea that a no-girl no-champagne customer taking up a strategic table all by himself in that jam-packed bedlam might not be the management's conception of a heaven-sent ghost. . . .

"Will there be anything else, sir?" asked a melancholy waiter suggestively, and the Saint stretched his long elegantly tailored legs as best he could in the few square inches allotted to him.

"No," he said. "But leave me your address, and if there is I'll write you a postcard."

The melancholy one flashed him a dark glance which suggested that his probable Sicilian ancestry was tempted to answer for him. But the same glance took in the supple width of the Saint's shoulders, and the rakish fighing lines of a face that was quite differently handsome from other good-looking faces that had sometimes strayed into Cookie's Cellar, and the hopeful mockery of translucent blue eyes which had a disconcerting air of being actively interested in trouble as a fine art; and for some reason he changed his mind. Whereby he revealed himself as the possessor of a sound instinct of self-preservation, if nothing else.

For those rather pleasantly piratical features had probably drifted in and out of more major forms of trouble than those of any other adventurer of this century. Newspaper reproductions of them had looked out from under headlines that would have been dismissed as a pulp writer's fantasy before the man whom they accoladed as the Robin Hood of modern crime arrived to make them real. Other versions of them could have been found in the police files of five continents, accompanied by stories and suspicions of stories that were no less startling if much more dull in literary style; the only thing lacking, from the jaundiced view-point of Authority, was a record of any captures and convictions. There were certain individual paladins of the Law, notably such as Chief Inspector Claud Eustace Teal, of Scotland Yard, and Inspector John Henry Fernack, of New York's Centre Street, whose pet personal nightmares were haunted by that impudent smile; and there were certain evil men who had thought that their schemes were too clever to be touched by justice who had seen those mocking blue eyes with the laughter chilling out of them, the last thing before they died.

And now so many of those things were only memories, and the Saint had new enemies and other battles to think of, and he sat in Cookie's Cellar with as much right and reason as any law-abiding citizen. Perhaps even with more; for he was lucky enough never to have heard of the place before a man named Hamilton in

Washington had mentioned it on the 'phone some days before.

Which was why Simon was there now with absolutely no intention of succumbing to the campaign of discouragement which had been waged against him by the head waiter, the melancholy waiter, the chef, and the chemist who measured out eye-droppers of cut liquor behind the scenes.

"Are you waiting for somebody, sir?" asked the melancholy waiter, obtruding himself again with a new variation on his primary motif; and the Saint nodded.

"I'm waiting for Cookie. When does she do her stuff?"

"It ain't hardly ever the same twice," said the man sadly. "Sometimes it's earlier and sometimes it's later, if you know what I mean."

"I catch the drift," said the Saint kindly.

The orchestra finally blew and banged itself to a standstill, and its component entities mopped their brows and began to dwindle away through a rear exit. The relief of relative quiet was something like the end of a barrage.

At the entrance across the room Simon could see a party of salesmen and their lighter moments expostulating with the head waiter, who was shrugging all the way down to his outspread hands with the unmistakable gesture of all head waiters who are trying to explain to an obtuse audience that when there is simply no room for any more tables there is simply no room for any more tables.

The melancholy waiter did not miss it either.

"Would you like your check, sir?" he inquired.

He put it down on the table to ease the decision.

Simon shook his head blandly.

"Not," he said firmly, "until I've heard Cookie. How

could I look my friends in the eye if I went home before that? Could I stand up in front of the Kiwanis
Club in Terre Haute and confess that I'd been to New
York, and been to Cookie's Cellar, and never heard her
sing? Could I face——?"

"She may be late," the waiter interrupted bleakly.
"She is, most nights."

"I know," Simon acknowledged. "You told me. Lately,
she's been later than she was earlier. If you know what I
mean."

"Well, she's got that there canteen, where she enter-
tains the sailors—and," added the glum one, with a
certain additionally defensive awe, "for free."

"A noble deed," said the Saint, and noticed the total
on the check in front of him with an involuntary twinge.
"Remind me to be a sailor in my next incarnation."

"Sir?"

"I see the spotlights are coming on. Is this going to
be Cookie?"

"Naw. She don't go on till last."

"Well, then she must be on her way now. Would you
like to move a little to the left? I can still see some of
the stage."

The waiter dissolved disconsolately into the shadows,
and Simon settled back again with a sigh. After having
suffered so much, a little more would hardly make any
difference.

A curly-haired young man in a white tuxedo appeared
at the microphone and boomed through the expectant
hush: "Ladies and gentlemen—Cookie's Cellar—welcomes you all again—and proudly presents—that sweet
singer of sweet songs . . . Miss—Avalon—Dexter! Let's
all give her a nice big hand."

We all gave her a nice big hand, and Simon took

another mouthful of his diluted ice-water and braced himself for the worst as the curly-haired young man sat down at the piano and rippled through the introductory bars of the latest popular pain. In the course of a reluctant but fairly extensive education in the various saloons and bistros of the metropolis, the Saint had learned to expect very little uplift, either vocal or visible, from sweet singers of sweet songs. Especially when they were merely thrown in as a secondary attraction to bridge a gap between the dance music and the star act, in pursuance of the best proven policy of night club management, which discovered long ago that the one foolproof way to flatter the intellectual level of the average *habitué* is to give him neither the need nor the opportunity to make any audible conversation. But the Saint felt fairly young, in fairly good health, and fairly strong enough to take anything that Cookie's Cellar could dish out, for one night at least, buttressing himself with the knowledge that he was doing it for his Country. . . .

And then suddenly all that was gone, as if the thoughts had never crossed his mind, and he was looking and listening in complete stillness.

And wondering why he had never done that before.

The girl stood under the single tinted spotlight in a simple white dress of elaborate perfection, cut and draped with artful artlessness to caress every line of a figure that could have worn anything or nothing with equal grace.

She sang:

> *"For it's a long, long time*
> *From May to December,*
> *And the days grow short*
> *When you reach November . . ."*

She had reddish-golden-brown hair that hung long over her shoulders and was cut straight across above large brown eyes that had the slightly oriental and yet not-oriental cast that stems from some of the peoples of eastern Europe. Her mouth was level and clean-cut, with a rich lower lip that warmed all her face with a promise of inward reality that could be deeper and more enduring than any ordinary prettiness.

Her voice had the harmonic richness of a 'cello, sustained with perfect mastery, sculptured with flawless diction, clear and pure as a bell.

She sang:

> *"And these few precious days*
> *I'd spend with you;*
> *These golden days*
> *I'd spend with you."*

The song died into silence; and there was a perceptible space of breath before the silence boiled into a crash of applause that the accompanist, this time, did not have to lead. And then the tawny hair was waving as the girl bowed and tossed her head and laughed; and then the piano was strumming again; and then the girl was singing again, something light and rhythmic, but still with that shining accuracy that made each note like a bubble of crystal; and then more applause, and the Saint was applauding with it, and then she was singing something else that was slow and indigo and could never have been important until she put heart and understanding into it and blended them with consummate artistry; and then again; and then once more, with the rattle and thunder of demand like waves breaking between the bars of melody, and the tawny mane tossing and her generous lips smiling;

and then suddenly no more, and she was gone, and the spell was broken, and the noise was empty and so gave up; and the Saint took a long swallow of scarcely flavoured ice-water and wondered what had happened to him.

And that was nothing to do with why he was sitting in a high-class clip joint like Cookie's Cellar, drinking solutions of Peter Dawson that had been emasculated to the point where they should have been marketed under the new brand name of Phyllis Dawson.

He looked at the dead charred end of a cigarette that he had forgotten a long time ago, and put it down and lighted another.

He had come there to see what happened, and he had certainly seen what happened.

The young piano-player was at the mike again, beaming his very professional beam.

He was saying: "And now—ladies and gentlemen—we bring you—the lady you've all been waiting for—in person—the one and only . . ."

"Lookie, lookie, lookie," said the Saint to himself, very obviously, but with the very definite idea of helping himself back to reality—"here comes Cookie."

2

As a raucous yowl of acclamation drowned out the climax of the announcement, Simon took another look at the table near the dais from which Cookie arose, if not exactly like Venus from the foam, at least like an inspired hippopotamus from a succulent wallow.

It was a table which he had observed during a previous casual survey of the room, without recognising Cookie herself as the third person who had joined it—a fact which the melancholy waiter, doubtless with malice aforethought, had carefully refrained from pointing out to him. But the two other people at it he had been able to place on the flimsier pages of a scrapbook memory.

The more feminine of the two, who wore the trousers, could be identified as a creature whose entrance to life had been handicapped by the name of Ferdinand Pairfield. To compensate for this, Mr. Pairfield had acquired a rather beautifully modelled face crowned with a mop of strikingly golden hair which waved with the regularity of corrugated metal, a pair of exquisitely plucked eyebrows arching over long-lashed soulful eyes, a sensuously chiselled mouth that always looked pink and shining as if it had been freshly skinned, and a variety of personal idiosyncrasies of the type which cause robustly ordinary men to wrinkle their nostrils. Simon Templar had no such commonplace reactions to personal whimsy; he had enough internal equanimity to concede any human being the right to indulge in any caprice that looked like fun to him, provided the caprice was confined to the home and did not discombobulate the general populace: but he did have a rather abstract personal objection to Ferdinand Pairfield. He disliked Mr. Pairfield because Mr. Pairfield had elected to be an artist, and moreover to be a very dexterous and proficient artist whose draughtsmanship would have won the approval of Dürer or Da Vinci. There was only one thing wrong with the Art of Ferdinand Pairfield. At some point in his development he had come under the influence of Dadaism, Surrealism, and Ultimate Googooism; with the result that he had never since then been able to paint a woman except with breasts that came out like bureau drawers, apexed with nipples that took the form of rattlesnakes, put-and-take tops, bottle-openers, shoe-horns, faucets, bologna sausage, or very small Packard limousines.

The other half of the duo was a gaunt, stringy-haired woman with hungry eyes and orange lipstick, whom he identified as Kay Natello, one of the more luminous of the most luminiscent modern poets. The best he could remember about her was a quote from a recent volume of hers, which might as well be reprinted here in lieu of more expensive descriptions:

FLOWERS

I love the beauty of flowers,
germinated in decay and excrement,
with soft slimy worms
crawling
caressingly
among the tender
roots.

So even I carry within me
decay and excrement:
and worms
crawl
caressingly
among the tender roots of my
love.

Between them they made a rather fine couple; and Simon realised how Cookie could have been the idol of both of them, if there were any foundation to the casual whispers he had been able to hear about her since he discovered that she was destined to enter his life whether he wanted it or not.

He looked for Cookie again, remembering that he was not there for fun.

She was sitting at the piano now, thumping the keys almost inaudibly while she waited for the informed applause to die away, with a broad and prodigiously hospitable smile on her large face.

She must have weighed more than two hundred and fifty pounds. The expansive grossness of her features was slightly minimised by a pompadoured convict coiffure which reduced the breadth of her face for as long as it lasted, but below that she was built like a corseted barrel. Her Brobdingnagian bosom bloused up from a skin of appalling sequins that shimmered down in recognisable ridges over the steatopygous scaffolding that encased her hips. As much as any other feature you noticed the hands that whacked uninhibitedly over the keyboard: large, splay-fingered, muscular, even with the incongruous vermilion lacquer on the nails they never looked like a woman's hands. They were the hands of a stevedore, a wrestler, or—for that matter —a strangler. They had a crude sexless power that narrowed down through the otherwise ludicrous excesses of her figure to give a sudden sharp and frightening meaning to the brash big-hearted bonhomie of her smile.

It was a strange and consciously exaggerated sensation that went through the Saint as he analysed her. He knew that some of it came from the electric contrast with the impression that Avalon Dexter had left on him. But he could make use of that unforeseen standard without letting it destroy his judgment, just as he could enlarge upon intuition only to see the details more clearly. He knew that there were not enough ingredients in the highballs he had drunk there to warp his intelligence, and he had never in his life been given to hysterical imaginings. And yet with complete dispassionate sanity, and no matter where it might go from there, he knew that for perhaps the first time in a life that had been crossed by many evil men he had seen a truly and eternally evil woman.

Just for a moment that feeling went over him like a dark wave; and then he was quite cool and detached again, watching her make a perfunctory adjustment to the microphone mounted in front of her.

"Hullo, everybody," she said in a deep commanding voice. "Sorry I'm late, but I've been taking care of some of our boys who don't get too much glory these days. I'm speaking of the plain ordinary heroes who man our merchant ships. They don't wear any brass buttons or gold braid, but war or no war they stay right on the job. The Merchant Navy!"

There was a clatter of approbation to show that the assembled revellers appreciated the Merchant Navy. It left no room for doubt that the hearts of Cookie's customers would always be in the right place, provided the place was far enough from the deck of an oil tanker to give them a nice perspective.

Cookie heaved herself up from the piano bench and pointed a dramatic finger across the room.

"And I want you to meet two of the finest men that ever sailed the seven seas," she roared. "Patrick Hogan and Axel Indermar. Take a bow, boys!"

The spotlight plastered two squirming youths at a side table, who scrambled awkwardly and unwillingly to their feet. Amid more spirited clapping, the spotlight switched back to Cookie as she sat down again and thumped out a few bars of *Anchors Aweigh* with a wide grin which charmingly deprecated her own share in bringing the convoy home.

"And now," she said, with a cascade of arpeggios,

"as a tribute to our guests of honour, let's start with *Testy Old William, the Nautical Man.*"

Overlapping a loyal diminuendo of anticipatory sniggers and applause from the initiated, she broadened her big jolly smile and launched into her first number.

Simon Templar only had to hear the first three lines to know that her act was exactly what he would have expected—a repertoire of the type of ballad which is known as "sophisticated" to people who like to think of themselves as sophisticated. Certainly it dealt with sundry variations on the facts of life which would have puzzled a clear-thinking farm hand.

It was first-class material of its kind, clever and penetrating to the thinnest edge of utter vulgarity; and she squeezed every last innuendo out of it as well as several others which had no more basis than a well-timed leer and the personal psychoses of the audience. There was no doubt that she was popular: the room was obviously peppered with a clique of regular admirers who seemed to know all her songs by heart, and who burst into ecstatic laughter whenever she approached a particularly classic line. Consequently, some of her finest gems were blanketed with informed hilarity—a fact which must have saved many an innocent intruder much embarrassment. But she was good; she had good material, she could sell it, she could get away with almost anything behind that big friendly bawdy boys-in-the-lavatory-together smile, and beyond any question she had more than enough of that special kind of showmanly bludgeoning personality that can pound an audience into submission and force them to admit that they have been wonderfully entertained whether they enjoyed it or not.

And the Saint hated her.

He hated her from a great distance; not because of
that first terrible but immaterial intuition, which was
already slipping away into the dimmer backgrounds of
his mind, nor in the very least because he was a prude,
which he was not.

He hated her because dominantly, sneakingly, overwhelmingly, phony-wittily, brazenly, expertly, loudly,
unscrupulously, popularly, callously, and evilly, with
each more ribald and *risqué* number that she dug out
of her perfertile gut, she was destroying and dissecting
into more tattered shreds a few moments of sweetness
and sincerity that a tawny-maned nobody named Avalon Dexter had been able to impose even on the tired
and tawdry café aristocracy who packed the joint. . . .

"I brought you a double, sir," said the melancholy
waiter, looming before him again in all the pride of a
new tactic. "Will that be all right?"

"That," said the Saint, "must have been what I was
waiting for all evening."

He controlled the pouring of water into the glass, and
tasted the trace of liquid in the bottom. It had a posi-
tive flavour of Scotch whisky which was nostalgically
fascinating. He conserved it respectfully on his palate
while Cookie blared into another encore, and looked
around to see whether by any chance there might be a
loose tawny mane anywhere within sight.

And, almost miraculously, there was.

She must have slipped out through another door,
but the edge of the spotlight beam clipped her head
for an instant as she bent to sit down. And that was
the instant when the Saint was looking.

The detail that registered on him most clearly was
the table where she sat. It was another ring-side table
only two spaces away from him, and it happened to be

one table which had never been out of the corner of his eye since he had accepted his own place. For it was the table of the one man whom he had really come there to see.

It gave him a queer feeling, somehow, after all that, to see her sitting down at the table of Dr. Ernst Zellermann.

Not that he had anything solid at all to hold against Dr. Zellermann—yet. The worst he could have substantially said about Dr. Zellermann was that he was a phony psychiatrist. And even then he would have been taking gross chances on the adjective. Dr. Zellermann was a lawful M.D. and a self-announced psychiatrist, but the Saint had no real grounds to insult the quality of his psychiatry. If he had been cornered on it, at that moment, he could only have said that he called Dr. Zellermann a phony merely on account of his Park Avenue address, his publicity, and a rough idea of his list of patients, who were almost exclusively recruited from a social stratum which is notorious for lavishing its diamond-studded devotion on all manner of mountebanks, yogis, charlatans, and magnaquacks.

He could have given equally unreasonable reasons why he thought Dr. Zellermann looked like a quack. But he would have had to admit that there were no proven anthropological laws to prevent a psychiatrist from being tall and spare and erect, with a full head of prematurely white and silky hair that contrasted with his smooth taut-skinned face. There was no intellectual impossibility about his wide thin-lipped mouth, his long thin aristocratic nose, or the piercing grey eyes so fascinatingly deep-set between high cheekbones and heavy black brows. It was no reflection on his professional qualifications if he happened to look exactly like any

Hollywood casting director's or hypochondriac society matron's conception of a great psychiatrist. But to the Saint's unfortunate scepticism it was just too good to be true, and he had thought so ever since he had observed the doctor sitting in austere solitude like himself.

Now he had other reasons for disliking Dr. Zeller-mann, and they were not at all conjectural.

For it rapidly became obvious that Dr. Ernst Zeller-mann's personal behaviour pattern was not confined to the high planes of ascetic detachment which one would have expected of such a perfectly-groomed mahatma. On the contrary, he was quite brazenly a man who liked to sit thigh to thigh with his companions. He was the inveterate layer of hands on knees, the persistent mauler of arms, shoulders, or any other flesh that could be conveniently touched. He liked to put heads together and mutter into ears. He leaned and clawed, in fact, in spite of his crisply patriarchal appearance, exactly like any tired business man who hoped that his wife would believe that he really had been kept late at the office.

Simon Templar sat and watched every scintilla of the performance, completely ignoring Cookie's progressively less subtle encores, with a concentrated and increasing resentment which made him fidget in his chair.

He tried, idealistically, to remind himself that he was only there to look around, and certainly not to make himself conspicuous. The argument seemed a little watery and uninspired. He tried, realistically, to remember that he could easily have made similar gestures himself, given the opportunity; and why was it romantic if he did it and revolting if somebody else did? This was manifestly a cerebral cul-de-sac. He almost persuaded himself that his ideas about Avalon Dexter were merely pyramided on the impact of her profes-

sional personality, and what gave him any right to
imagine that the advances of Dr. Zellermann might
be unwelcome?—especially if there might be a diamond
ring or a nice piece of fur at the inevitable conclusion
of them. And this very clearly made no sense at all.

He watched the girl deftly shrug off one paw after
another, without ever being able to feel that she was
merely showing a mechanical adroitness designed to
build up ultimate desire. He saw her shake her head
vigorously in response to whatever suggestions the vul-
turine wizard was mouthing into her ear, without being
able to wonder if her negative was merely a technical
postponement. He estimated, as cold-bloodedly as it was
possible for him to do it, in that twilight where no one
else might have been able to see anything, the growing
strain that crept into her face, and the mixture of shame
and anger that clouded her eyes as she fought off Zellermann as unobtrusively as any woman could have
done. . . .

And he still asked nothing more of the night than a
passable excuse to demonstrate his distaste for Dr. Ernst
Zellermann and all his works.

And this just happened to be the heaven-sent night
which would provide it.

As Cookie reached the climax of her last and most
lurid ditty, and with a sense of supremely fine predes-
tination, the Saint saw Avalon Dexter's hand swing
hard and flatly at the learned doctor's smoothly shaven
cheek. The actual sound of the slap was drowned in
the ecstatic shrieks of the cognoscenti who were antici-
pating the tag couplet which their indeterminate ancestors had howled over in the First World War; but
to Simon Templar, with his eyes on nothing else, the
movement alone would have been enough. Even if he

had not seen the girl start to rise, and the great psychologist reach out and grab her wrist.

He saw Zellermann yank her back on to her chair with a vicious wrench, and carefully put out his cigarette.

"*Nunc dimittis*," said the Saint, with a feeling of ineffable beatitude creeping through his arteries like balm; "O Lord, now lettest thou thy servant depart in peace. . . ."

He stood up quietly, and threaded his way through the intervening tables with the grace of a stalking panther, up to the side of Dr. Ernst Zellermann. It made no difference to him that while he was on his way Cookie had finished her last number, and all the lights had gone on again while she was taking her final bows. He had no particular views at all about an audience or a lack of it. There was no room in his soul for anything but the transcendent bliss of what he was going to do.

Almost dreamily, he gathered the lapels of the doctor's dinner jacket in his left hand and raised the startled man to his feet.

"You really shouldn't do things like that," he said in a tone of kindly remonstrance.

Dr. Zellermann stared into sapphire blue eyes that seemed to be laughing in a rather strange way, and some premonitive terror may have inspired the wild swing that he tried to launch in reply.

This, however, is mere abstract speculation. The recordable fact is that Simon's forearm deflected its fury quite effortlessly into empty air. But with due gratitude for the encouragement, the Saint proceeded to hit Dr. Zellermann rather carefully in the eye. Then, after steadying the healer of complexes once more by his coat lapels, he let them go in order to smash an equally

careful left midway between Dr. Zellermann's nose and
chin.

The psychiatrist went backwards and sat down suddenly in the middle of a grand clatter of glass and
china; and Simon Templar gazed at him with deep
scientific concern.

"Well, well, well," he murmured. "What perfectly
awful reflexes!"

3

For one fabulous moment there was a stillness and
silence such as Cookie's Cellar could seldom have ex-
perienced during business hours; and then the background noises broke out again in a new key and tempo,
orchestrated with a multiplying rattle of chairs as the
patrons in the farther recesses stood up for a better
view, and threaded with an ominous bass theme of the
larger waiters converging purposefully upon the centre
of excitement.

The Saint seemed so unconcerned that he might
almost have been unaware of having caused any dis-
turbance at all.

He said to Avalon Dexter: "I'm terribly sorry—I
hope you didn't get anything spilt on you."

There was an unexpected inconsistency of expression in the way she looked at him. There were the remains of pardonable astonishment in it, and a definite
shadowing of fear; but beyond that there was an in-
finitesimal curve in the parted lips which held an incongruous hint of delight.

She said in a rather foolish and meaningless way:
"Thank you——"

Then the vanguard of the sedative squad was at the
Saint's side, in the person of a captain whose face looked

as if it had known rougher employment than smirking welcomes and farewells to transient suckers.

He was a fairly weighty man, and his tuxedo was tight across his shoulders. He grasped the Saint's arm and said without any professional servility: "What's this all about?"

"Just a little apache dance routine," Simon said pleasantly. "Unscheduled addition to the floor show. I've been practising it quite a while. Would you like me to show you, or would you rather let go my arm?"

The bouncer captain, with the Saint's biceps palpably under his fingers and the Saint's very cool blue eyes on him, seemed to experience a shred of indecision.

Avalon Dexter's clear voice said: "Take it easy, Joe."

Simon gently eased his arm away in the act of searching for a cigarette, and gazed interestedly at Dr. Zellermann, who was trying to unwrap himself from a tablecloth with which he had become entangled in the course of his descent.

"Unfortunately," he explained, "my partner hasn't practised so much, and his timing is all off. It's too bad he had to fall down and hurt his face, but accidents will happen."

Dr. Zellermann got to his feet, assisted by one of the larger waiters, who thoughtfully kept hold of him under the guise of continuing his support.

With his patriarchal locks dishevelled, one eye closed, and a smear of blood smudged down from one corner of his mouth, Dr. Zellermann was not in the least beautiful or benign. In fact, for a man who claimed to adjust the mental disorders of others, he showed a lamentable lack of psychic balance. He spoke to and about the Saint, in very precise English mingled with a few recherché foreign epithets and expletives; and Simon was saddened to learn from the discourse that the doctor was clearly the victim of several psychoses, inclined towards paranoia, subject to perverse delusions, and afflicted with obsessive coprophilia. Simon realised that the symptoms might have been aggravated by some recent shock, and he was considering the case with clinical impartiality when Cookie herself surged through the ring of bystanders.

Simon had never thought she was beautiful, but now he saw for himself how ugly she could look. The big practised smile was gone, and her mouth was as hard and functional as a trap. Her eyes were bright, watchfully venomous, and coldly capable. For that moment, in spite of the complete appositeness of all the associations, Simon felt that she had the identical bearing of a hard-boiled matron preparing to quell trouble in a tough reform school.

"What's this all about?" she demanded, using what began to sound like the house formula.

"This insolent swine," Zellermann said, gathering his words with a vicious precision that made them come out as if he were spitting bullets, "attacked me for no reason at all——"

"Or only one little reason," said the Saint easily. "Because I saw you grab Miss Dexter's arm, and I thought you were getting much too rough."

"Because she slapped me!"

"For a very good reason, chum. I saw it."

Cookie's wet marble eyes flicked from face to face with the alertness of a crouched cat surrounded by sparrows. Now she turned on the girl.

"I see," she rasped. "What have you been drinking, Avalon?"

Simon admired the blushless pot-and-kettle majesty
of that, for at close quarters Cookie was enveloped in a
rich aroma of whisky which probably contributed some
of the beady glaze to her malevolent stare.

"Really Cookie," he said earnestly, "anyone who
wanted to get tight on the drinks you serve here would
have to have been working on it since breakfast."

"Nobody asked you to come here," Cookie threw
at him, and went on to Avalon: "I'd like to know what
the hell makes you think you've got a right to insult
my customers——"

It was not a pretty scene, even though the Saint's
aversion to that kind of limelight was greatly tempered
by the happy memory of his knuckles crushing Dr.
Zellermann's lips against his teeth. But he felt much
more embarrassed for Avalon. The puzzling hint of
a smile had left her lips altogether, and something else
was coming into her eyes that Cookie should have been
smart enough to recognise even if she was too alcoholic
for ordinary discretion.

He said quietly: "The customer insulted her,
Cookie——"

"You dirty liar!" shouted Zellermann.

"——and he had it coming to him," Simon went on
in the same tone. "I saw it all happen. Why not just
throw him out and let's go on with the fun?"

"You mind your own goddam business!" Cookie
blazed at him purply. Again she turned to the girl. "You
drunken slut—I've had just about enough of your airs
and graces and bull——"

That was it. Avalon's lips came together for an instant, and the suppressed blaze flashed like dynamite
in her eyes.

"That's fine," she said. "Because I've had just about

enough of you and your creep joint. And as far as I'm concerned you can take your joint and your job and stuff them both."

She whirled away; and then after only one step she turned back, just as abruptly, her skirts and her hair swooping around her. And as she turned she was really smiling.

"That is," she added sweetly, "if the Saint doesn't do it for you."

Then she was gone, sidling quickly between the tables; and there was a new stillness in the immediate vicinity.

In the local silence, the Saint put a match to his neglected cigarette.

Now he understood the paradoxical ingredient in Avalon's expression when she first saw him. And her revelation flared him into an equally paradoxical mixture of wariness and high amusement. But the barest lift of one eyebrow was the only response that could be seen in his face.

Cookie's stare had come back to him, and stayed there. When she spoke to him again her voice had no more geniality than before, and yet there was still a different note in it.

"What's your name?"

"Simon Templar," he said, with no more pointedness than if he had said "John Smith."

The effect, however, was a little different.

The muscular captain took a step back from him, and said with unconscious solemnity: "Jesus!"

Dr. Ernst Zellermann stopped mopping his mouth with a reddening handkerchief, and kept still like a pointer.

Cookie kept still too, with her gross face frozen in

the last expression it had worn, and her eyes so anchored that they looked almost rigid.

The Saint said peaceably: "It's nice to have met you
all, but if somebody would give me my check I'd like
to get some fresh air."

The melancholy waiter was at his side like a lugu-
brious genie, holding up the check by the time he had
finished his sentence.

"Now, just a minute, Mr. Templar." Cookie's voice
came through again with the sticky transparency of
honey poured over a file. "These little things do happen in night clubs, and we all understand them. I didn't
mean to be rude to you—I was just upset. Won't you
sit down and have a drink with me?"

"No, thank you," said the Saint calmly. "I've already
had several of your drinks, and I want to get my tummy
pumped out before goldfish start breeding in it."

He peeled a bill off his roll and handed it to the
waiter with a gesture which dismissed the change.

"Of course you thought you were doing the right
thing," Cookie persisted. "But if you only knew the
trouble I've had with that little tramp, I'm sure——"

"I'm quite sure," said the Saint, with the utmost
charm, "that I'd take Avalon's suggestion—and throw
Dr. Zellermann in for a bonus."

He turned on his heel and sauntered away—he
seemed tired of the whole thing and full of time to
spare, but that effect was an illusion. He wanted very
much indeed to catch Avalon Dexter before he lost her,
and his long lazy stride took him to the door without
a wasted movement.

The check-room girl was helping him into his coat
when Ferdinand Pairfield, on his way to the gents'
room, edged past him at a nervous distance that was

not without a certain coy concupiscence. The Saint reached out and took his hand.

"Don't you think that nail polish is a bit on the garish side, Ferdy?" he asked gravely. "Something with a tinge of violet in it would look much cuter on you."

Mr. Pairfield giggled, and disengaged his fingers as shyly and reluctantly as a débutante.

"Oh, *you*!" he carolled.

Slightly shaken, Simon let himself out and went up the short flight of steps to the street.

Avalon Dexter was on the sidewalk, talking to the doorman as he held the door of a taxi for her. Even with her back to him, the Saint couldn't have mistaken the long bronze hair that hung over the shoulders of her light wolf coat. She got into the cab as he reached the street level; and before the doorman could close the door Simon took two steps across the pavement, ducked under the man's startled nose, and sat down beside her.

He held out a quarter, and the door closed.

She gazed at him in silence.

He gazed at her, smiling.

"Good morning," she said. "This is cosy."

"I thought I might buy you a drink somewhere," he said, "and wash the taste of that dump out of our mouths."

"Thanks," she said. "But I've had all I can stand of creep joints for one night."

"Then may I see you home?"

Her candid eyes considered him for a bare moment. "Why not?"

She gave the driver an address on Sutton Place South.

"Do you make all that money?" Simon asked interestedly, as they moved off.

"The place I've got isn't so expensive. And I work pretty regularly. At least," she added, "I used to."

"I hope I didn't louse everything up for you."

"Oh, no. I'll get something else. I was due for a change anyway. I couldn't have taken much more of Cookie without going completely nuts. And I can't think of any happier finale than to-night."

Simon stretched out to rest his heels on the folding seat opposite him, and drew another eighth of an inch off his cigarette.

He said idly: "That was quite an exit line of yours."

"They got the idea, did they?"

"Very definitely. You could have heard a pin drop. I heard one."

"I'd give a lot to have seen Cookie's face."

"She looked rather like a frog that was being goosed by an electric eel."

The girl laughed quickly; and then she stopped laughing.

"I hope I didn't louse everything up for you."

"Oh, no." He doubled her tone exactly as she had doubled his. "But it was just a little unexpected."

"For a great detective, you've certainly got an awful memory."

He arched an eyebrow at her.

"Have I?"

"Do you remember the first crossing of the *Hindenburg*—the year before it blew up?" She was looking straight ahead, and he saw her profile intermittently as the dimmed street lights touched it. "You were on board—I saw your picture in a newsreel when you arrived. Of course, I'd seen pictures of you before, but that reminded me. And then a couple of nights later you were in a place called the Bali, opposite El Morocco.

Jim Moriarty had it—before he had the Barberry Room. I was bellowing with the band there, and you came in and sat at the bar." She shrugged, and laughed again. "I must have made a tremendous impression."

He didn't remember. He never did remember, and he never ceased to regret it. But it was one of those things.

He said lamely: "I'm sorry—that was a lot of years ago, and I was crashing all over town and seeing so many people, and I can't have been noticing much."

"Oh, well," she said, with a stage sigh. "Dexter the Forgotten Girl. What a life! . . . And I thought you came to my rescue to-night because you remembered. But all the time you were taken up with so many people that you never even saw me."

"I'm sorry," he said again. "I must have been taken up with too many people. And I'll never forgive any of them."

She looked at him, and her smile was teasing and gay, and her eyes were straight and friendly with it, so that it was all only chatter and she was not even trying to sell him anything; and he could only smile back and think how much better it could have been if he remembered.

"Maybe you don't know how lucky you were," she said.

"Maybe I don't," he said.

And it was a curious thing that he only half understood what he was saying, or only half meant what he said; it was only a throw-away line until after it was spoken, and then it was something that could never be thrown away.

This was something that had never been in his mind at all when he abandoned himself to the simple enjoyment of smacking Dr. Ernst Zellermann in the smooch.

He lighted another cigarette with no less care than he had devoted to the other operation, and said nothing more until the taxi drew up outside a black and white painted brick building on the river side of Sutton Place South. He got out and helped her out, and she said: "Come in for a minute and let me fix you a real drink."

"That's just what I needed," he said, and paid off the taxi, and strolled up beside her as casually as if they had known each other for a hundred years, and it was just like that, and that was how it was.

4

The living-room was at the back. It was big and quiet and comfortable. There was a phono-radio and a record cabinet, and a big bookcase, and another tier of shelves stacked with sheet music, and a baby piano. The far end of it was solid with tall windows.

"There's a sort of garden outside," she said. "And the other end of it falls straight down on to East River Drive, and there's nothing beyond that but the river, so it's almost rustic. It only took me about three years to find it."

He nodded.

"It looks like three well-spent years."

He felt at home there, and easily relaxed. Even the endless undertones of traffic were almost lost there, so that the city they had just left might have been a hundred miles away.

He strolled by the bookcase, scanning the titles. They were a patchwork mixture, ranging from *The African Queen* to *The Wind in the Willows*, from Robert Nathan to Emil Ludwig, from *Each to the Other* to

Innocent Merriment. But they made a pattern, and in a little while he found it.

He said: "You like some nice reading."

"I have to do something with my feeble brain every so often. I may be just another night-club singer, but I did go to Smith College and I did graduate from University of California, so I can't help it if I want to take my mind off creep joints sometimes. It's really a great handicap."

He smiled.

"I know what you mean."

He prowled on, came to the piano, set his drink on it, and sat down. His fingers rippled over the keys, idly and aimlessly, and then crept into the refrain of *September Song.*

She sat on the couch, looking at him, with her own glass in her hand.

He finished abruptly, picked up his drink again, and crossed the room to sit down beside her.

"What do you know about Zellermann?" he asked.

"Nothing much. He's one of these Park Avenue medicine-men. I think he's supposed to be a refugee from Vienna—he got out just before the Nazis moved in. But he didn't lose much. As a matter of fact, he made quite a big hit around here. I haven't been to his office, but I'm told it looks like something off a Hollywood set. His appointment book looks like a page out of the Social Register, and there's a beautifully carved blonde nurse-receptionist who'd probably give most of his male patients a complex if they didn't have any to start with. He's got a private sanatorium in Connecticut, too, which is supposed to be quite a place. The inmates get rid of their inhibitions by doing exactly what they please and then paying for any special damage."

"You mean if they have a secret craving to tear the clothes off a nurse or throw a plate of soup at a waiter, they can be accommodated—at a fancy tariff."

"Something like that, I guess. Dr. Zellermann says that all mental troubles come from people being thwarted by some convention that doesn't agree with their particular personality. So the cure is to take the restriction away—like taking a tight shoe off a corn. He says that everyone ought to do just what their instincts and impulses tell them, and then everything would be lovely."

"I noticed he wasn't repressing any of his impulses," Simon remarked.

The girl shrugged.

"You're always meeting that sort of creep in this sort of business. I ought to have been able to handle him. But what the hell. It just wasn't my night to be tactful."

"You'd met him before, of course."

"Oh, yes. He's always hanging around the joint. Cookie introduced him the other night. He's one of her pets."

"So I gathered. Is it Love, or is he treating her? I should think a little deep digging into her mind would really be something."

"You said it, brother. I wouldn't want to go in there without an armoured diving suit."

He cocked a quiet eye at her.

"She's a bitch, isn't she?"

"She is."

"Everybody's back-slapper and good egg, with a heart of garbage and scrap iron."

"That's about it. But people like her."

"They would." He sipped his drink. "She gave me rather a funny feeling. It sounds so melodramatic, but she's the first woman I ever saw who made me feel that she was completely and frighteningly evil. It's a sort of psychic feeling, and I got it all by myself."

"You're not kidding. She can be frightening."

"I can see her carrying a whip in a white-slave trading post, or running a baby farm and strangling the little bastards and burying them in the back yard."

Avalon laughed.

"You mightn't be so far wrong. She's been around town for years, but nobody seems to know much about her background before that. She may have done all those things before she found a safer way of making the same money."

Simon brooded for a little while.

"And yet," he said, "the waiter was telling me about all the public-spirited work she does for the sailors."

"You mean Cookie's Canteen? . . . Yes, she makes great character with that."

"Is it one of those Seamen's Missions?"

"No, it's all her own. She hands out coffee and cake and sandwiches, and there's a juke box and hostesses and entertainment."

"You've been there, I suppose."

"I've sung there two or three times. It's on Fiftieth Street near Ninth Avenue—not exactly a ritzy neighbourhood, but the boys go there."

He put a frown and a smile together, and said: "You mean she doesn't make anything out of it? Has she got a weakness for philanthropy between poisonings, or does it pay off in publicity, or does she dote on those fine, virile uninhibited sailor boys?"

"It could be all of those. Or perhaps she's got one last leathery little piece of conscience tucked away somewhere, and it takes care of that and makes her feel really fine. Or am I being a wee bit romantic? I don't know. And what's more, I don't have to care any more, thank God."

"You're quite happy about it?"

"I'm happy anyway. I met you. Build me another drink."

He took their glasses over to the side table where the supplies were, and poured and mixed. He felt more than ever that the evening had been illumined by a lucky star. He could put casual questions and be casually flippant about everything, but he had learned quite a lot in a few hours. And Cookie's Canteen loomed in his thoughts like a great big milestone. Before he was finished with it he would want more serious answers about that irreconcilable benevolence. He would know much more about it and it would have to make sense to him. And he had a soft and exciting feeling that he had already taken more than the first step on the unmarked trail that he was trying to find.

He brought the drinks back to the couch, and sat down again, taking his time over the finding and preparation of a cigarette.

"I'm still wondering," she said, "what anyone like you would be doing in a joint like that."

"I have to see how the other half lives. I'd been out with some dull people, and I'd just gotten rid of them, and I felt like having a drink, and I happened to be passing by, so I just stopped in."

None of it was true, but it was good enough.

"Then," he said, "I heard you sing."

"How did you like it?"

"Very much."

"I saw you before I went on," she said. "I was singing for you."

He struck a match, and went on looking at her between glances at the flame and his kindling cigarette.

He said lightly: "I never knew I was so fascinating."

"I'm afraid you are. And I expect you've been told all about it before."

"You wouldn't like me if you knew me."

"Why not?"

"My glamour would dwindle. I brush my teeth just like anyone else; and sometimes I burp."

"You haven't seen me without my make-up."

He inspected her again critically.

"I might survive it."

"And I'm lazy and untidy, and I have expensive tastes."

"I," he said, "am not a respectable citizen. I shoot people and I open safes. I'm not popular. People send me bombs through the mail, and policemen are always looking for an excuse to arrest me. There isn't any peace and stability where I'm around."

"I'm not so peaceful and stable myself," she said seriously. "But I saw you once, and I've never forgotten you. I've read everything about you—as much as there is to read. I simply knew I was going to meet you one day, even if it took years and years. That's all. Well, now I've met you, and you're stuck with it."

She could say things like that, in a way that nobody else could have said them and gotten away with it. The Saint had met most kinds of coquetry and invitation, and he had had to dodge the anthropophagous pursuit of a few hungry women: but this was none of those things. She looked him in the face when she said it, and she said it straight out as if it was the most natural thing to say because it was just the truth; but there was a little speck of laughter in each of her eyes at the

same time, as if she wondered what he would think of
it and didn't care very much what he thought.

He said: "You're very frank."

"You won't believe me," she said, "but I never told
anyone anything like this before in my life. So if
you think I'm completely crazy you're probably
right."

He blew smoke slowly through his lips and gazed at
her, smiling a little but not very much. It was rather
nice to gaze at her like that, with the subdued lamplight
on her bronze head, and feel that it was the most obvious
and inescapable thing for them to be doing.

This was absurd, of course; but some absurdities were
more sure than any commonplace probabilities.

He picked up his glass again. He had to say something, and he didn't know what it would be.

The door-bell beat him to it.

The shrill, tinny sound ripped shockingly through
his silence, but the lift of his brows was microscopic.
And her answering grimace was just as slight.

"Excuse me," she said.

She got up and went down the long hall corridor. He
heard the door open, and heard a tuneless contralto
voice that twanged like a flat guitar string.

"Hul-*lo, darling!*—oh, I'm so glad I didn't get you
out of bed. Could I bring the body in for a second?"

There was the briefest flash of a pause, and Avalon
said: "Oh, sure."

The door latched, and there was movement.

The raw clock-spring voice said audibly: "I'm not
butting in, am I?"

Avalon said flatly: "Of course not. Don't be silly."

Then they were in the room.

The Saint unfolded himself off the couch.

"Mr. Templar," Avalon said. "Miss Natello. Simon—Kay."

"How do you do?" said the Saint, for want of a better phrase.

"Come in, Kay," Avalon said. "Sit down and make yourself miserable. Have a drink? You know what this night life is like. The evening's only just started. What goes on in the big city?"

Her gay babble was just a little bit forced, and perhaps only the Saint's ears would have noticed it.

Kay Natello stayed in the entrance, plucking her orange-painted mouth with the forefinger and thumb of one hand. Under her thick sprawling eyebrows, her haunted eyes stared at the Saint with thoughtful intensity.

"Mr. Templar," she said. "Yes, you were at Cookie's."

"I was there," said the Saint vaguely, "for a while."

"I saw you."

"Quite a big night, wasn't it?" Avalon said. She sank back on to the settee. "Come on in and have a drink and tell us your troubles. Simon, fix something for her."

"I won't stay," Kay Natello said. "I didn't know you had company."

She hauled her angular bony frame out of its lean-to position against the entrance arch as gauchely as she put her spoken sentences together.

"Don't be so ridiculous," Avalon said. She was impatiently hospitable—or hospitably impatient. "We were just talking. What did you come in for, if you didn't want to stay for a few minutes?"

"I had a message for you," Kay Natello said. "If Mr. Templar would excuse us . . ."

"If it's from Cookie, Mr. Templar was part of the ruckus, so it won't hurt him to hear it."

The other woman went on pinching her lower lip with skeletal fingers. Her shadowed eyes went back to the Saint with completely measurable blankness, and back to Avalon again.

"All right," she said. "I didn't mean to crash in here at all, really, but Cookie made such a fuss about it. You know how she is. She was a bit tight, and she lost her temper. Now she's getting tighter because she shouldn't have. She'd like to forget the whole thing. If you could . . . sort of . . . make it up with her . . ."

"If she feels like that," Avalon said, with that paralysing smiling directness which was all her own, "why didn't she come here herself?"

"She's too tight now. You know know she gets. But I know she's sorry."

"Well, when she sobers up, she can call me. She knows where I live."

"I know how you feel, darling. I only stopped in because she begged me to. . . . I'll run along now."

Avalon stood up again.

"Okay," she said, with friendly exhaustion. "I've taken a lot from Cookie before, but to-night was just too much—that's all. Why don't you beat some sense into her one of these times when she's receptive?"

"You know how she is," Kay Natello said, in that metallic monotone. "I'm sorry."

She hitched her wrap up once again around her scrawny shoulders, and her hollow eyes took a last deliberate drag at the Saint.

"Good night, Mr. Templar," she said. "It was nice meeting you."

"It was nice meeting you," Simon replied, with the utmost politeness.

He crossed to the side table again and half refilled

his glass while he was left alone, and turned back to
meet Avalon Dexter as the outer door closed and her
skirts swished through the entrance of the room again.

"Well?" She was smiling at him, as he was convinced now that nobody else could smile. "How do you
like that?"

"I don't," he said soberly.

"Oh, she's as whacky as the rest of Cookie's clique,"
she said carelessly. "Don't pay any attention to her. It's
just like Cookie to try and send an ambassador to do
her apologising for her. It'd hurt too much if she ever
had to do it herself. But just this once I'm not going
to——"

"I'm afraid you've missed something," Simon said,
still soberly, and perhaps more deliberately. "Natello
didn't come here to deliver Cookie's apologies. I've got
to tell you that."

Avalon Dexter carried her glass over to the side
table.

"Well, what did she come for?"

"You went out with a beautiful exit line. Only it was
just too good. That's why Cookie is so unhappy now.
And that's why she had Natello drop in. To find out
what kind of a hook-up there might be between us.
It happens that there wasn't any." The Saint put his
glass transiently to his mouth. "But that isn't what
Natello found out."

The break in her movements might have been no
more than an absent-minded search for the right bottle.

"So what?" she asked.

"So I honestly didn't mean to involve you with anything," he said.

She completed the reconstruction of a high-ball without any other hesitation; but when she turned to him

again with the drink in her hand, the warm brown eyes
with the flecks of laughter in them were as straight as he
had always seen them.

"Then," she said, "you didn't just happen to be at
Cookie's to-night by accident."

"Maybe not," he said.

"For Heaven's sake, sit down," she said. "What is
this—a jitterbug contest? You and Kay ought to get
married. You could have so much fun."

He smiled at her again, and left one final swallow in
his glass.

"I've got to be running along. But I'm not fooling.
I really wish to hell that nobody who had any connection with Cookie had seen me here. And now, to
use your own words, you're stuck with it."

She looked at him with all the superficial vivacity
thrown off, seriously, from steady footholds of maturity.
And like everything else she did that was unexpected,
after she had done it it was impossible to have expected
anything else.

"You mean it might be—unhealthy?"

"I don't want to sound scary, but . . . yes."

"I'm not scared. But don't you think you might tell
me why?"

He shook his head.

"I can't, right now. I've told you more than I should
have already, as a matter of fact. But I had to warn
you. Beyond that, the less you know, the safer you'll
be. And I may be exaggerating. You can probably
brush it off. You recognised me from a picture you saw
once, and you were good and mad, so you threw out that
parting crack just to make trouble. Then I picked you
up outside, and you thought I'd been nice, so you just
bought me a drink. That's the only connection we have."

"Well, so it is. But if this is something exciting, like the things I fell in love with you for, why can't I be in on it?"

"Because you sing much too nicely, and the ungodly are awful unmusical."

"Oh, fish," she said.

He grinned, and finished his drink, and put down the glass.

"Throw me out, Avalon," he said. "In another minute dawn is going to be breaking, and I'm going to shudder when I hear the crash."

And this was it, this was the impossible and inevitable, and he knew all at once now that it could never have been any other way.

She said: "Don't go."

CHAPTER TWO

How Dr. Zellermann used the Telephone and Simon Templar went visiting

SIMON woke up with the squeal of the telephone bell splitting his eardrums. He reached out a blind hand for it and said: "Hullo."

"Hullo," it said. "Mr. Templar?"

The voice was quite familiar, although its inflexion was totally different from the way he had heard it last. It was still excessively precise and perfectionist; but whereas before it had had the precision of a spray of machine-gun slugs, now it had the mellifluous authority of a mechanical unit in a production line.

"Speaking," said the Saint.

"I hope I didn't wake you up."

"Oh, no."

Simon glanced at his wrist-watch. It was just after twelve.

"This is Dr. Ernst Zellermann," said the telephone.

"So I gathered," said the Saint. "How are you?"

"Mr. Templar, I owe you an apology. I had too much to drink last night. I'm usually a good drinker, and I have no idea why it should have affected me that way. But my behaviour was inexcusable. My language—I would prefer to forget. I deserved just what happened to me. In your place, I would have done exactly what you did."

The voice was rich and crisp with candour. It was the kind of voice that knew what it was talking about, and automatically inspired respect. The professional voice. It was a voice which naturally invited you to bring it your troubles, on which it was naturally comfortable to lean.

Simon extracted a cigarette from the pack on the bedside table.

"I knew you wouldn't mind," he said amiably. "After all, I was only carrying out your own principles. You did what your instincts told you—and I let my instincts talk to me."

"Exactly. You are perfectly adjusted. I congratulate you for it. And I can only say I am sorry that our acquaintance should have begun like that."

"Think nothing of it, dear wart. Any other time you feel instinctive we'll try it out again."

"Mr. Templar, I'm more sorry than I can tell you. Because I have a confession to make. I happen to be one of your greatest admirers. I have read a great deal about you, and I've always thought of you as the ideal exponent of those principles you were referring to. The man who never hesitated to defy convention when he knew he was right. I am as detached about my own encounter with you as if I were a chemist who had been blown up while he was experimenting with an explosive. Even at my own expense, I have proved myself right. That is the scientific attitude."

"There should be more of it," said the Saint gravely.

"Mr. Templar, if you could take that attitude yourself, I wish you would give me the privilege of meeting you in more normal circumstances."

The Saint exhaled a long streamer of smoke towards the ceiling.

"I'm kind of busy," he said.

"Of course, you would be. Let me see. This is Thursday. You are probably going away for the week-end."

"I might be."

"Of course, your plans would be indefinite. Why don't we leave it like this? My number is in the telephone book. If by chance you are still in town on Saturday, would you be generous enough to call me? If you are not too busy, we might have lunch together. How is that?"

Simon thought for a moment, and knew that there was only one answer.

"Okay," he said. "I'll call you."

"I shall be at your disposal."

"And by the way," Simon said gently, "how did you know my 'phone number?"

"Miss Dexter was kind enough to tell me where you were staying," said the clipped persuasive voice. "I called her first, of course, to apologise to her. . . . Mr. Templar, I shall enjoy resuming our acquaintance."

"I hope you will," said the Saint.

He put the handpiece back, and lay stretched out on his back for a while with his hands clasped behind his head and his cigarette cocked between his lips, staring uncritically at the opposite cornice.

He had several things to think about, and it was a queer way to be reminded of them—or some of them —item by item, while he was waking himself up and trying to focus his mind on something else.

He remembered everything about Cookie's Cellar, and Cookie, and Dr. Ernst Zellermann, and everything else that he had to remember; but beyond that there was Avalon Dexter, and with her the memory went into a strange separateness like a remembered dream, unreal and incredible and yet sharper than reality and belief. A tawny mane and straight eyes and soft lips. A voice singing. And a voice saying: "I was singing for you . . . the things I fell in love with you for . . ."

And saying: "Don't go. . . ."

No, that was the dream, and that hadn't happened.

He dragged the telephone book out from under the bedside table, and thumbed through it for a number.

The hotel operator said: "Thank you, sir."

He listened to the burr of dialling.

Avalon Dexter said: "Hello."

"This is me," he said.

"How nice for you." Her voice was sleepy, but the warm laughter was still there. "This is me, too."

"I dreamed about you," he said.

"What happened?"

"I woke up."

"Why don't you go back to sleep?"

"I wish I could."

"So do I. I dreamed about you, too."

"No," he said. "We were both dreaming."

"I'd still like to go back to sleep. But creeps keep calling me up."

"Like Zellermann, for instance?"

Yes. Did he call you?"

"Sure. Very apologetic. He wants me to have lunch with him."

"He wants *us* to have lunch with him."

"On those terms, I'll play."

"So will I. But then, why do we have to have him along?"

"Because he might pick up the check."

"You're ridiculous," she said.

He heard her yawn. She sounded very snug. He could almost see her long hair spread out on the pillow.

"I'll buy you a cocktail in a few hours," he said, "and prove it."

"I love you," she said.

"But I wasn't fooling about anything else I said last night. Don't accept any other invitations. Don't go to any strange places. Don't believe anything you're told. After you got yourself thought about with me last night, anything could happen. So please be careful."

"I will."

"I'll call you back."

"If you don't," she said, "I'll haunt you."

He hung up.

But it had happened. And the dream was real, and it was all true, and it was good that way. He worked with his cigarette for a while.

Then he took the telephone again, and called room service. He ordered corned beef hash and eggs, toast and marmalade and coffee. He felt good. Then he revived the operator and said: "After that you can get me a call to Washington. Imperative five, five hundred. Extension five. Take your time."

He was towelling himself after a swift stinging shower when the bell rang.

"Hamilton," said the receiver dryly. "I hope you aren't getting me up."

"This was your idea," said the Saint. "I have cased the joint, as we used to say in the soap operas. I have inspected your creeps. I'm busy."

"What else?"

"I met the most wonderful girl in the world."

"You do that every week."

"This is a different week."

"This is a priority line. You can tell me about your love life in a letter."

"Her name is Avalon Dexter, and she's in the directory. She's a singer, and until the small hours of this morning she was working for Cookie."

"Which side is she on?"

"I only just met her," said the Saint, with unreal impersonality. "But they saw her with me. Will you remember that, if anything funny happens to me—or to her? . . . I met Zellermann, too. Rather violently, I'm afraid. But he's a sweet and forgiving soul. He wants to buy me a lunch."

"What did you buy last night?" Hamilton asked suspiciously.

"You'll see it on my expense account—I don't think it'll mean raising the income tax rate more than five per cent.," said the Saint, and hung up.

He ate his brunch at leisure, and saved his coffee to go with a definitive cigarette.

He had a lot of things to think about, and he only began trying to co-ordinate them when the coffee was clean and nutty on his palate, and the smoke was crisp on his tongue and drifting in aromatic clouds before his face.

Now there was Cookie's Canteen to think about. And that might be something else again.

Now the dreaming was over, and this was another day.

He went to the closet, hauled out a suit-case, and threw it on the bed. Out of the suit-case he took a bulging brief-case. The brief-case was a particularly distinguished piece of luggage, for into its contents had gone an amount of ingenuity, corruption, deception, seduction, and simple larceny which in itself could have supplied the backgrounds for a couple of dozen stories.

Within its hand-sewn compartments was a collection of documents in blank which represented the cream of many years of research. On its selection of letterheads could be written letters purporting to emanate from almost any institution between the Dozey Dairy Company of Kansas City and the Dominican Embassy in Ankara. An assortment of visiting cards in two or three crowded pockets was prepared to identify anybody from the Mayor of Jericho to Sam Schiletti, outside plumbing contractor, of Exterior Falls, Oregon. There were passports with the watermarks of a dozen governments —driving licences, pilot's licences, ration books, credit cards, birth certificates, warrants, identification cards, passes, permits, memberships, and authorisations enough to establish anyone in any rôle from a Bulgarian tightrope walker to a wholesale fish merchant from Grimsby. And along with them there was a unique symposium of portraits of the Saint, flattering and unflattering, striking and nondescript, natural and disguised—together with a miscellany of stamps, seals, dies, and stickers which any properly conditioned bureaucrat would have drooled with ecstasy to behold. It was an outfit that would have been worth a fortune to any modern brigand, and it had been worth exactly that much to the Saint before.

He sat down at the desk and worked for an un-hurried hour, at the end of which time he had all the necessary documents to authenticate an entirely imagin-ary seaman by the name of Tom Simons, of the British Merchant Marine. He folded and refolded them several times, rubbed the edges with a nail file, smeared them with cigarette ash, sprinkled them with water and a couple of drops of coffee, and walked over them several times until they were convincingly soiled and worn.

Then he finished dressing and went out. He took a Fifth Avenue bus to Washington Square, and walked from there down through the grey shabby streets of the lower east side until he found the kind of store he was looking for.

He couldn't help the natural elegance of his normal appearance, but the proprietor eyed him curiously when he announced himself as a buyer and not a seller.

"I've got a character part in a play," he explained, "and this was the only way I could think of to get the right kind of clothes."

That story increased his expenses by at least a hun-dred per cent.; but he came out at the end of an hour with an untidy parcel containing a complete out-fit of well-worn apparel that would establish the charac-ter of Tom Simons against any kind of scrutiny.

He took a taxi back to the Algonquin.

There were two telephone messages.

Miss Dexter 'phoned, and would call again about seven o'clock.

Miss Natello 'phoned.

Simon arched his brows over the second message, and

smiled a little thinly before he tore it up. The ungodly were certainly working. Fundamentally he didn't mind that, but the persistence of the coverage took up the slack in his nerves. And it wasn't because he was thinking about himself.

He called Avalon's number, but there was no answer.

There are meaningless gulfs of time in real life which never occur in well-constructed stories—hours in which nothing is happening, nothing is about to happen, nothing is likely to happen, and nothing does happen. The difference is that in a story they can be so brightly and lightly skimmed over, simply by starting a fresh paragraph with some such inspired sentence as "Simon Templar went downstairs again for a drink, and Wolcott Gibbs waved to him across the lobby, and they spent a couple of congenial hours lamenting the sad standards of the current season on Broadway."

Simon Templar went downstairs again for a drink, and Wolcott Gibbs waved to him across the lobby, and they spent a couple of congenial hours lamenting the sad standards of the current season on Broadway; and all the time Simon was watching the clock and wondering what held back the hands.

It was fifteen hours, or minutes, after seven when the call came.

"Merry Christmas," she said.

"And a happy new year to you," he said. "What goes?"

"Darling," she said, "I forgot that I had a date with my arranger to go over some new songs. So I had to rush out. What are you doing?"

"Having too many drinks with Wolcott Gibbs."

"Give him my love."

"I will."

"Darling," she said, "there's a hotel man from Chicago in town—he used to come and hear me bellow when I was at the Pump Room—and he wants me to go to dinner. And I've got to find myself another job."

He felt empty inside, and unreasonably resentful, and angry because he knew it was unreasonable.

"I'm sorry," he said.

"So am I. I do want to see you, really."

"Have you met this creep before?"

"Oh, yes. Lots of times. He's quite harmless—just a bit dreary. But he might have a job for me, and I've got to earn an honest living somehow. Don't worry— I haven't forgotten what you told me about being careful. By the way, you'll be glad to hear Cookie called me."

"She did?"

"Yes. Very apologetic, and begging me to drop in and see her."

"What are you going to do?"

"I don't know. I hate the joint and I hate her, but she knows everybody in town and she isn't a good enemy to have. I'll see what happens to-night. . . . What are you going to be doing later?"

"Probably carousing in some gilded cesspool, surrounded by concubines and champagne."

"I ought to be able to get rid of this creep at a sensible hour, and I would like to see you."

"Why don't you call me when you get through? I'll probably be home. If I'm not, leave a number."

"I will." Her voice was wistful. "Don't be too gay with those concubines."

Simon went back to his table. He felt even emptier inside. It had been such a beautiful dream. He didn't know whether to feel foolish, or cynical, or just careless. But he didn't want to feel any of those things. It was a persistent irritation, like a piece of gravel in a shoe.

"What are you doing this evening?" Gibbs asked him.

"Having another drink."

"I've got to get some dinner before I go to that opening. Why don't you join me?"

"I'd like to." Simon drained his glass. He said casually: "Avalon Dexter sent you her love."

"Oh, do you know her? She's a grand gal. A swell person. One of the few honest-to-God people in that racket."

There was no doubt about the spontaneous warmth of Wolcott's voice. And measured against his professional exposure to all the chatter and gossip of the show world, it wasn't a comment that could be easily dismissed. The back of Simon's brain went on puzzling.

2

The Saint watched Mr. Gibbs depart, and gently tested the air around his tonsils. It felt dry. He moved to the cusp of the bar and proceeded to contemplate his nebulous dissatisfactions.

He ordered more of the odious product of the house of Dawson and meditated upon the subject of Dr. Ernst Zellermann, that white-maned, black-browed high priest of the unconscious mind.

Why, Simon asked himself, should a man apologise for sticking his face in the way of a fast travelling fist? Why should Dr. Z. wish to further his acquaintance of the Saint, who had not only knocked him tail over tea-kettle but had taken his charming companion home? How, for that matter, did Dr. Z. know that Avalon

Dexter might have the telephone number of Simon Templar?

Beyond the faintest shadow of pale doubt, Brother Zellermann was mixed up in this situation. And since the situation was now the object of the Saint's eagle eyeing, the type-case psychiatrist should come in for his share of scrutiny. And there was nothing to do but scrutinise. . . .

Simon tossed off everything in his glass but a tired ice cube, and went out into the night. The doorman flicked one glance at the debonair figure who walked as if he never touched the ground, and almost dislocated three vertebræ as he snapped to attention.

"Taxi, sir?"

"Thanks," said the Saint, and a piece of silver changed hands. The doorman earned this by crooking a finger at a waiting cab driver. And in another moment Simon Templar was on his way to the Park Avenue address of Dr. Zellermann.

It was one of those impulsive moves of unplanned exploration that the Saint loved best. It had all the fascination of potential surprises, all the intriguing vistas of an advance into new untrodden country, all the uncertainty of dipping the first fork into a plate of roadside eating stew. You went out into the wide world and made your plans as you went along and hoped the gods of adventure would be good to you.

Simon relaxed hopefully all the way up-town until the taxi decanted him in front of the windowed monolith wherein Dr. Ernst Zellermann laved the libido.

A light burned on the twelfth floor, and that was entrée even though the lobby roster placed Dr. Zellermann on the eighteenth floor. Simon entered the elevator, signed "John Paul Jones" on the form for nocturnal visitors, said "Twelve" to the ancient lackey, and was levitated on greased runners.

He walked toward the lighted doorway, an emporium of Swedish masseurs, but wheeled on silent feet as soon as the elevator doors closed and went up six flights as swiftly and as silently as the elevator had ascended. The lock on Zellermann's door gave him little trouble, snicking open to reveal a waiting-room of considerable proportions.

The pencil beam of his flashlight told him that the man who decorated this restful room knew the value of the pause that relaxes. "This is your home," the room said. "Welcome. You like this chair? It was made for you. The prints? Nice, aren't they? Nothing like the country. And isn't that soft green of the walls pleasant to the eye? Lean back and relax. The doctor will see you presently, as a friend. What else, in these surroundings?"

The Saint tipped his mental hat and looked around for more informative detail. This wasn't much. The receptionist's desk gave up nothing but some paper and pencils, a half pack of cigarettes, a lipstick, and a copy of *Trembling Romances*. Three names were written on an appointment pad on the desk top.

He went into the consultation room, which was severely furnished with plain furniture. A couch lay against one wall, the large desk was backed against an opaque window, and the walls were free of pictorial distractions.

Yet this, too, was a restful room. The green of the reception-room walls had been continued here, and despite the almost monastic simplicity of the *décor*, this room invited you to relax. Simon had no doubt that a patient lying on the couch, with Dr. Zellermann discreetly in the background gloom, would drag from the censored files of memory much early minutiæ, the stuff of which human beings are made.

But where were the files? The office safe?

Surely it was necessary to keep records, and surely the records of ordinary daily business need not be hidden. The secretary must need a card file of patients, notations, statements of accounts, and what not.

Once more the pencil beam slid around the office, and snapped out. Then the Saint moved silently—compared to him, a shadow would have seemed to be wearing clogs—back into the reception room. His flash made an earnest scrutiny of the receptionist's corner and froze on a small protuberance. Simon's fingers were on it in a second. He pulled, then lifted—and a section of wall slid upward to reveal a filing cabinet, a small safe, and a typewriter.

The Saint sighed as he saw the aperture revealed no liquid goods. Tension always made him thirsty, and breaking and entering always raised his tension a notch.

As he reached for the top drawer of the file to see what he could see, the telephone on the reception desk gave out a shrill demand. The Saint's reflexes sent a hand toward it, which hovered over the instrument while he considered the situation. More than likely, somebody had called a wrong number. It was about that time in the evening when party goers reach the point where it seems a good idea to call somebody, and the somebody is often determined by spinning the dial at random.

If it happens to be your telephone that rings, and you struggle out of pleasant dreams to curse any dizzy friend who would call you at that hour, and you say "Hello" in churlish tones, some oafish voice is likely as not to give you a song and a dance about being a telephone tester, and would you please stand three feet away from the 'phone and say "Methodist Episcopalian" or some such phrase, for which you get the horse laugh when you pick up the 'phone again.

This is considered top-hole wit in some circles.

If this were the case, Simon reflected, no harm could be done by answering. But what harm in any case? he asked himself, and lifted the receiver.

"Hullo."

"Ernst?" asked a sharp and vaguely familiar voice. "I'm glad you came early. I'll be there immediately. Something has arisen in connection with Gamaliel Foley."

Click. The caller hung up. That click was echoed by the Saint's memory, and he directed his flashlight at the appointment pad to confirm it. There it was, sandwiched between the names of Mrs. Gerald Meldon and James Prather. Gamaliel Foley.

The Saint was torn between two desires. One was to remain and eavesdrop on the approaching meeting of Dr. Z. and his caller with the vaguely familiar voice; the other was to find Gamaliel Foley and learn what he could learn. The latter procedure seemed more practical, since the office offered singularly few conveniences for eavesdropping; but Simon was saddened by the knowledge that he would never know what happened when the conferees learned that it was not Dr. Zellermann who had answered the call.

He replaced the wall panel and went away. On the twelfth floor he summoned the elevator, and he wasn't certain whether or not he hoped he wouldn't encounter Park Avenue's psyche soother. It might have been an interesting passage at charms, for the doctor could give persiflage with the best. But no such contretemps occurred on the way out; and Simon walked the block to Lexington Avenue and repaired to a drug-store stocked with greater New York's multiple set of telephone directories.

He found his man, noted the Brooklyn address, and hailed a taxicab.

For a short while Simon Templar gave himself over to trying to remember a face belonging to the voice that had spoken with such urgency on the telephone. The owner of the voice was excited, which would distort the voice to some extent; and there was the further possibility that Simon had never heard the voice over the telephone before, which would add further distortion to remembered cadences and tonal qualities.

His worst enemies could not call Simon Templar methodical. His method was to stab—but to stab unerringly—in the dark. This characteristic, possessed to such an incredible degree by the Saint, had wrought confusion among those same worst enemies on more occasions than can be recorded here—and the list wouldn't sound plausible, anyway.

So, after a few unsatisfactory sallies into the realm of Things To Be Remembered, he gave up and leaned back to enjoy the ride through the streets of Brooklyn. He filed away the incident under unfinished business and completely relaxed. He gave no thought to his coming encounter with Gamaliel Foley, of which name there was only one in all New York's directories, for he had no referent. Foley, so far as he was concerned, might as well be Adam, or Zoroaster—he had met neither.

When the cab driver stopped at the address the Saint had given, Simon got out and walked back two blocks to the address he wanted. This was an apartment house of fairly respectable mien, a blocky building rising angularly into some hundred feet of midnight air. Its face was pocked with windows lighted at intervals, and its whole demeanour was one of middle-class stolidity.

He searched the name-plates beside the door, found Foley on the eighth floor. The Saint sighed again. This was his night for climbing stairs. He rang a bell at random on the eleventh floor, and when the door buzzed, slipped inside. He went up the carpeted stairway, ticking off what the residents had had for dinner as he went. First floor, lamb, fish, and something that might have been beef stew; second floor, cabbage; third floor, ham flavoured with odours of second floor's cabbage; and so on.

He noted a strip of light at the bottom of Foley's door. He wouldn't be getting the man out of bed, then. Just what he would say, Simon had no idea. He always left such considerations to the inspiration of the moment. He put knuckles to the door.

There was no sound of a man getting out of a chair to grump to the door in answer to a late summons. There was no sound at all. The Saint knocked again. Still no sound. He tried the door. It opened on to a living-room modestly furnished with medium-priced over-stuffed pieces.

"Hullo," Simon called softly. "Foley?"

He stepped inside, closed the door. No one was in the living-room. On the far side was a door leading into a kitchen, the other no doubt led into the bedroom. He turned the kitchen light on, looked about, switched off the light and knocked on the bedroom door. He opened it, flicked the light switch.

There was someone here, all right—or had been. What was here now was not a person, it was a corpse. It sprawled on the rug, face down, and blood had

seeped from the back to the dark green carpet. It was—
had been—a man.

Without disturbing the body any more than necessary, Simon gathered certain data. He had been young,
somewhere in his thirties; he was a white-collar worker,
neat, clean; he bore identification cards which named
him Gamaliel Bradford Foley, member of the Seamen's Union.

The body bore no information which would link this
man with Dr. Ernst Zellermann. Nor did the apartment,
for that matter. The Saint searched it expertly, so that
it seemed as if nothing had been disturbed, yet every
possible hiding-place had been thoroughly explored.
Foley, it seemed, was about to become engaged to a Miss
Martha Lane, Simon gathered from a letter which he
shamelessly read. The comely face which smiled from
a picture on Foley's dresser was probably her likeness.

Since no other information was to be gathered here,
the Saint left. He walked a half-dozen blocks to a
crowded all-night drug-store, and went into an empty
'phone booth, where he dialled Brooklyn police.

He told the desk sergeant that at such and such an
address "you will find one Gamaliel Foley, F-o-l-e-y,
deceased. You'll recognise him by the knife he's wearing—in his back."

3

At the crack of ten-thirty the next morning, Avalon
Dexter's call brought him groggily from sleep.

"It's horribly early," she said, "but I couldn't wait
any longer to find out if you're all right."

"Am I?" the Saint asked.

"I think you're wonderful. When do you want to see
me?"

"As soon as possible. Yesterday, for example. Did you have a good time last night?"

"Miserable. And you?"

"Well, I wouldn't call it exciting. I thought about you at odd moments."

"Yes, I know," she said. "Whenever you did, I turned warm all over, and wriggled."

"Must have been disconcerting to your escort."

She laughed, bells at twilight.

"It cost me a job, I think. He'd peer at me every time it happened. I think he concluded it was St. Vitus. The job was in Cleveland, anyway."

"Some of the best people live in Cleveland," Simon said.

"But you don't, so I didn't go."

"Ordinarily, I'd have a nice fast come-back for such a leading remark, but I seem to have trouble finding any words at all."

"You could say 'I love you'."

"I love you," Simon said.

"Me, too, kid."

"This being Friday," Simon said, "what do you say we go calling on people after we have brunched together, and then let the rest of the day take care of itself?"

"That scrambling sound," she said, "is eggs in my kitchen. So hurry."

"Thirty minutes," said the Saint, and hung up.

He had never needed thirty minutes to shave, shower, and dress, but he needed to make a call.

Hamilton said: "What kind of a jam are you in this time?"

"If you can get anything on one Gamaliel Bradford Foley," the Saint said, "it might be useful. I'd do it myself, but you can do it faster, and I expect to be sort of busy on other things."

"What sort of other things?"

"I'm going to read the papers, and take my girl calling."

"The same girl?"

"But definitely," said the Saint.

"What have you learned?"

"Nothing," the Saint said, "that is of any specific use to us, but the wind is full of straws. I'm watching to see how they fall."

"I trust you know the difference between straws and hay," Hamilton said somewhat darkly, and rang off.

Simon picked up a paper on the way out of the hotel, and found the death of Gamaliel Bradford Foley recorded in two paragraphs on an inside page.

DEATH LOOKS IN ON TOP SEAMEN'S UNION OFFICIAL

Gamaliel Bradford Foley, secretary of the Seamen's Union, Local 978 (AFL), was found stabbed to death in his Brooklyn apartment early this morning by police.

A telephone tip—"You'll recognise him by the knife he's wearing—in his back"—sent patrol car 12 to the scene. Officers J. R. McCutcheon and I. P. Wright found the corpse in the apartment bedroom, with a butcher knife in its back. An arrest is expected any moment, Inspector Fernack told reporters to-day.

It wasn't a smile that twisted the Saint's sensitive mouth as the taxi took him to Avalon's place—it was a grimace of scepticism. "An arrest is expected any moment." He shrugged. The police certainly knew no more than himself—not as much, as a matter of fact. He knew of the connection, however nebulous, between

Foley and Dr. Zellermann. How could the police expect an arrest?

Ah, well. That was the sort of thing reporters put on copy paper. City editors had to be considered, too. If you, as a reporter, 'phoned your desk with a story, you wanted something to lead into a follow-up yarn, and "arrest expected" certainly indicated more to come.

Avalon met him in a housecoat of greenish blue that in a strange and not understandable way was completely right for her. She turned up her face and he kissed her on the mouth, that mouth so full of promise. They said nothing.

She led him to a divan, where he sat wordless with her beside him. Her tawny hair was shot with glints of gold. Her eyes, he noted in passing, were dark, yet alight. He thought of a title by Dale Jennings: "Chaos Has Dark Eyes."

She said: "Hullo, boy."

He grinned.

"I burgle joints and discover bodies. I am not a respectable character. You wouldn't like me if you knew me."

"I know you," she said. "I like you. I'll demonstrate —later."

She got up, went into the kitchen, and brought back a bottle of beer.

"I hope you belong to the beer-for-breakfast school."

"There's nothing like it, unless it's Black Velvet. But that's for special breakfasts."

"Isn't this?"

"Well, not quite, you must admit."

"Yes, I must admit." She gave him a smile, a short kiss. "Excuse me while I make eggs perform."

He sipped his beer and wondered about Mrs. Gerald

Meldon, whose Park Avenue address he had decided to visit. Gerald Meldon was a name to conjure with in Wall Street. He was at one time the Boy Wonder of the mart. If he went for a stock, it signalled a rush of hangers-on. This had caused him to operate under pseudonyms, which the Saint considered having a touch of swank—a stock-market operator using phony names. If Meldon were known to be dumping a stock, this was another signal. Everybody who could get hold of the information dumped his. The stock usually went down.

It had been Gerald Meldon, the son—obviously—of a rich father, who had made collegiate history by dressing in white coveralls, driving along Fifth Avenue, and stealing all the street lamp bulbs one afternoon. It had been Gerald Meldon who had been chosen by Grantland Rice as All-American tackle from Harvard, accent and all.

The Saint knew nothing of Mrs. Gerald Meldon, but he could understand that reasons might exist why she should seek psychiatric help from Dr. Z. Well, he would see what he would see.

It was easy enough to find Meldon's address in the directory, and after breakfast that was what he did.

When he and Avalon arrived there later—she was now in a tailored suit of tan gabardine—the first thing he saw caused him to clutch her arm.

"Sorry," he muttered, "but my eyes have suddenly gone back on me."

She put a hand on his. Her dark eyes clouded.

"What is it, darling?"

"I'm seeing things. It must have been the beer."

She followed his gaze.

"I'm seeing things too."

"Surely not what I'm seeing. Describe to me carefully what you think you see."

"Well, there's a kind of liveried slave on the end of a dog leash. Then, on the other end of the leash is a mink coat, and inside the coat is a dachshund. The man is leading the dog—or vice versa—from, er, pillar to post."

The Saint sighed explosively.

"If you see it, too, there's nothing wrong with me, I guess."

The sad-faced little dog led the liveried attendant nearer. The dog wagged its tail at them, the attendant elevated his nose a trifle.

"Doesn't the little beast find that a trifle warm, this time of year?" he asked the attendant.

"It isn't a question of warmth, sir—it's—ah, shall we say face? He's a Meldon property, you know."

Simon could detect no trace of irony in tone or attitude.

"But—mink? A trifle on the ostentatious side?"

"What else, sir?" asked the gentleman's gentleman.

The Saint rang the doorbell. He and Avalon were presently shown into the drawing-room, furnished in chrome and leather, lightened by three excellent Monets, hooded in red velvet drapes. Mrs. Meldon came to them there.

She was most unexpected. She did not conform. She was beautiful, but not in the fashion affected by the house. Hers was an ancient beauty, recorded by Milton, sung by Sappho. She was tall and dark. Her hair reminded you of Egyptian princesses—black and straight, outlining a dark face that kings might have fought for. She walked with an easy flowing motion in high heels that accentuated a most amazing pair of slim ankles and exciting legs. These latter were bare and brown.

Her dress was of some simple stuff, a throw-away factor until you saw how it high-lighted such items as should be high-lighted. It clung with loving care to her hips, it strutted where it should strut. She had a placid smile, dark eyes brightened with amusement, and a firm handshake.

Her voice held overtones of curiosity. "You wanted to see me?"

The Saint introduced himself.

"I am Arch Williams, a researcher for *Time* magazine. This is my wife."

"Quite a dish," Mrs. Meldon said. "I'll bet you play hell with visiting firemen. I'm very happy to meet you. Drink? Of course. You look the types."

Her teeth, the Saint noted, were very white. She rang a bell with a brown hand. A servant appeared.

"Move the big bar in here, Walker." To the Saint: "Those monkey suits kill me. Gerry thinks they're necessary. Prestige, you know." She made the phrase sound like unacceptable language from a lady. "*Time*, hmm? What do you want from me? Never mind, yet. Wait'll we get a drink. You have lovely legs, Mrs. Williams."

"Thank you."

"Oh, don't thank me. I had nothing to do with it. But they are pretty. I hope your husband appreciates them. So many don't."

The Saint said nothing. He wanted to watch.

"I think he appreciates them," Avalon murmured. "Don't you, dear?"

Simon smiled.

"So many don't," Mrs. Meldon said. "You can pour

yourself into a sheer tube of a dress, like mine, and a husband will look at you, glance at his watch, and give you hell for being thirty minutes late. My God, how do men expect us to make ourselves—— Oh, here are the drinks. Name your poison."

When they had drinks, Mrs. Meldon gave the Saint a slow smile.

"Well, Mr. Researcher, what now?"

"I have been assigned to find out what I can about Dr. Ernst Zellermann. We're going to pick a Doc of the Year. No slow-poke, medicine, you know."

Mrs. Meldon stared at him.

"My God, you talk in that style! Don't you find it nauseating?"

"I quit," Simon said. "But could I ask you a few questions, Mrs. Meldon? We've picked some possible subjects from the professional standpoint, and it's my job to find out what their patients think of them."

"Why pick on me?"

"You're a patient of Dr. Zellermann's?"

"Well—uh, yes."

The Saint filed her hesitation away for future reference.

"How do you like him?" he asked.

"He's rather colossal, in a nauseating way."

"So? I should think a feeling of that sort would hamper the—er—rapport between doctor and patient."

"Oh, it does," she said, "no end. He wishes I'd like him. A phony, he."

"Really? I thought he was quite reputable."

"What is reputable?" Mrs. Meldon countered. "Is it what empty-headed bitches say who are suckers for a patriarchal look and soft hands? Is it what some jerk says—'Five hundred dollars I paid, for a single inter-

view'—after he's stung? He has an M.D., so what?
I know an abortionist who has one."

"It helps," said the Saint.

"What do you want to know about him?" Mrs. Meldon asked. "When he was three years old in Vienna,
a butcher slapped his hands because he reached for a
sausage. As a result he puts his nurse in a blue smock.
He won't have a white uniform around him. He doesn't
know this, of course. He has no idea that the butcher's
white apron caused a psychic trauma. He says he in-
sists on blue uniforms because they gladden the eyes."

"He begins to sound like not our kind of man," the
Saint put in.

"Oh, go ahead and pick him," said the Egyptian
princess. "Who the hell cares? He wouldn't be the first
mass of psychic trauma picked as an outstanding jerk.
No inhibitions, says he. It's a little tough on somebody
who's put inhibitions by the board for these many
moons to go to him as a patient. Shooting fish down a
barrel, I calls it. Another drink? Of course. Mix it
yourself."

She crossed her lovely legs in such a fashion that a
good portion of thigh was visible. She didn't bother to
pull down her dress. She seemed tired of the discussion, even a trifle embittered, and a pattern began to
form in the Saint's mind. He put early conclusions aside
in the interest of conviviality and mixed drinks.

"Tell me," he said, "how you expect to get psychiatric help from a man you hold in such disregard?"

She straightened up.

"Disregard? Nothing of the sort. He knows the patter,
he has the desk-side manner. He can make you tell
things about yourself you wouldn't tell yourself. Maybe it helps, I don't know. Yes, I must admit it does.

It helped me to understand myself, whatever small consolation that may be. I didn't want to understand myself. But Gerry insisted. He wants to keep up with things. Like mink coats on dogs."

"You would say, then, that your relations with Dr. Zellermann have been pleasant?"

She looked at him steadily as he handed her a drink. "Pleasant? What's that? Sometimes you get caught up in an emotion. Emotion is a driving power you can't ignore. When you get caught up in it, whatever you do seems pleasant at the time. Even if you curse yourself afterwards, and even if you don't dare talk about it."

"Do you mean, then, he isn't ethical?"

She twisted a smile.

"What's ethical? Is being human ethical? You're born human, you know. You can't help certain impulses. See Freud. Or Krafft-Ebing. To err is human."

"And he errs?"

"Of course he does. Even if he is a so-called witch doctor of the mind. Even if he has studied Adler and Brill and Jung and Jones. You don't change a character. All the things that went into making him what he is are unalterable. They've happened. Maybe some of his professors, or fellow psychiatrists, have helped him to evaluate those factors in their proper perspective, but he's still *homo sapiens* and subject to the ills they're heir to."

The Saint drank his drink, set the empty glass on the elaborate portable bar.

"We've taken enough of your time. Thanks for being so helpful."

Mrs. Meldon rose to her full and lovely height. "I'm no cross section on the man. Many more think he's wonderful than not. And in some ways," she said thoughtfully, "he's quite a guy, I guess."

The Saint did not ask what those ways were. He took himself and Avalon away, and hailed a taxi. When they were in it, and he had given the address of James Prather to the driver, he let himself consider Mrs. Meldon.

"Blackmail," he said finally.

"Ah, beg pardon?" Avalon murmured. "Understanding not."

"It's in the picture somewhere," he insisted. "I don't care how free from inhibition she may be, she wouldn't be as bitter as she was unless he's bleeding her in some fashion. How, is the question."

"I don't expect to be of any help," Avalon said meekly, "but I suspect the lady has played fast and loose at one time or another with the doctor—or others."

"Could be," Simon answered. "And you are a help, you know, just by being."

That line of thought occupied them shamelessly during the remainder of the ride.

James Prather they found to occupy an expensive flat in an expensive neighbourhood. He gave them a rather nervous welcome, bade them be seated, and did not offer a drink. James Prather paced the floor in house slippers, smoking-jacket, and fawn-coloured slacks. He was a man middling thirty, with great blue eyes that reminded you of a lobster. His chin was a hue, neither pale nor blue.

He twisted the question out between writhing fingers. "Yes? What is it?"

The Saint represented himself again as a *Time* magazine man, and named the subject of his research.

"Yes, yes," Prather said. "What about Dr. Zeller-mann? What kind of a man, or what kind of a doctor?"

"Both," said the Saint.

"Ah, well——" The telephone rang. "Excuse me." Prather answered, listened intently for a moment. Then he shot a glance at the Saint. "Yes," he said. "Yes. I see. Good-bye."

He turned to Simon. "Will you please get out of here?"

The Saint watched Mr. Prather at first with a mild disdain, as if he were watching a caterpillar in some-body else's salad; then with mild amusement, as if he had discovered the owner of the salad to be his dip-somaniac Uncle Lemuel; then with concern, as if he had remembered that Uncle Lem was without issue, and might leave that hand-painted cuff-link to his only nephew; then with resignation, as if it were suddenly too late to rescue Uncle—or the caterpillar.

Simon motioned Avalon to a tasteful divan, and seated himself. His eyes were now mocking and gay, with blue lights. His smile was as carefree and light as a lark at dawn. He took a gold pencil and a pad from his pocket.

"You were saying," he prompted, "about Dr. Zeller-mann?"

James Prather's fingers were like intertwined pallid snakes, writhing in agony.

"Please," he begged. "You must go at once. I have no time for you now. Come back to-morrow, or next week. An important appointment, unexpected. Sorry, but——"

He went to the door, and held it open.

The Saint considered, and after due and deliberate consideration rose and helped Avalon to her feet.

"I'd like to come back," he told Prather at the door. Prather nodded nervously, watched the Saint and Avalon walk toward the elevator for a few feet, then almost slammed the door. Simon pushed the elevator button and, just before the door opened, planted a swift kiss on her startled but quickly responsive mouth.

"Wait for me in the lobby, darling," he whispered, and handed her inside the car.

He took up a post of observation farther down the hall, so that the elevator door was half-way between him and Prather's door. He suspected he would not have long to wait before something happened. What that something might be, he was unable to predict.

He thought of the false trails he had run down before he began to sniff around Cookie's Cellar. He wondered if this would turn out to be another. Each of his previous attempts to locate the object of his search had uncovered one or more nests of illegality.

One had led him to a sort of warehouse, a huge structure where vast numbers of bottles of bona-fide liquors were made less intoxicating by the simple addition of faintly coloured distilled water. All very healthful, no doubt, and tending to reduce the incidence of drunkenness among habitués of clip clubs like Cookie's—where, incidentally, one of the delivery trucks had led him. This wholesale watering of drinks had another humanitarian aspect: it saved work for the bar-tenders. Still, when he remembered the quality of Cookie's drinks, the Saint concluded that she and/or her bartenders had initiative along that same line. The Saint felt that there was room for reasonable doubt that the reduction of the alcoholic potency of the drinks stemmed from compassionate motives, cynical though that conclusion might be.

Another trail had dragged across it a herring that had turned out to be the numbers racket. During his brief examination of exponents of mathematical larceny, he had been led again, by one of the collectors, to Cookie's.

He had run down a couple of false leads that led nowhere except to the decision that this was Mecca for the chiseller, and that some of almost everybody's best friends are petty crooks at bottom.

The Saint was looking for bigger game. Perhaps the rising elevator would bring some.

It regurgitated two young men who were beyond doubt fresh in from the sea. They wore shore clothes, but the sea was in their tanned faces, their hard hands, and the set of their legs, braced automatically for the roll of a deck. The Saint couldn't see their eyes in the hall's gloom, but he knew they would have the characteristic look of those who gaze habitually on circular horizons.

They walked without speaking to James Prather's door, thumbed the button, were admitted. The Saint moved cat-like to the door, but listening brought nothing. The door was heavy, the walls designed to give privacy to the occupant. Simon sighed, summoned the elevator, and joined Avalon, who was sitting in one of those chairs that clutter the lobbies of apartment houses and gazing at the uninspiring wallpaper with a forlorn expression.

"I beg your pardon, Miss," he said, "but I was attracted by your beauty, and can't help asking you a question. I am a representative of Grimes Graphite, Inc.—'Grimes' gets the grime,' you know—and felt certain that you must use it. Is that what makes your skin glow so?"

"My mother before me, and her mother before her, rubbed their faces each night with Grimes's graphite. But I don't use it myself. I loathe it."

"That is hardly the point at issue, is it? We can use that line about your maternal progenitors, run a photo of yourself—do you ski?—no matter, we can fix that. And we might even be persuaded to raise the ante."

"You twisted my bank-book," Avalon said. "I'm your gal."

"Really?"

She smiled. "Really."

They looked at each other for a long moment, until several persons came through the front door in a group, of which the male members stared at Avalon with very obvious admiration. The Saint took her outside.

"An idea has slugged me," he said, "and I don't want you to be seen talking to me until we're ready. I just hope our sailor boys give me a couple of minutes to tell you."

"What are you talking about?" she demanded as he hailed a passing taxi.

He helped her in.

"Wait," he told the driver, and closed the glass panel separating the production end of the cab from the pay-load.

"I have a faint hunch," he told Avalon in a low voice. "Two young men will presently issue from that door. Possibly you saw them come in. Tanned, one in a fresh-pressed grey suit, the other in blue? Did they notice you?"

"Looked right through me."

"Don't be bitter, darling. They had big things on their minds. On their way down, they'll be free of care and ready to paint the town. On the way down, they'll remember you, and would be anxious to spend their newly-acquired wealth on you."

"I don't know what you're talking about."

By not so much as the twitch of a nerve did the Saint reveal his thoughts. He had not talked too much; he never talked too much. But if Avalon were among the Ungodly—and his every red corpuscle stood up on its hind feet and howled at the thought—she would know whether he was breathing hard on the heels of truth or not. Her knowledge would then be communicated to the Boys Above.

He hoped, and was not prepared to admit even to himself how much he hoped, that his shadowy objectivity had no foundation in fact. But in his unorthodox plan of manœuvring, a failure to appraise situations and people with a fishy eye often led to the filling of mourners' benches. He'd helped to fill a few himself in his day.

And so the smile he gave Avalon was gay as confetti on New Year's Eve.

"I'm not so sure, old thing, that I myself know what I'm talking about. But if I do, those boys will come out of there with one single first desire: transportation to celebration. And I'd rather they kept greedy eyes off our cab." He opened the glass panel. "Pull up to the corner and wait," he told he driver.

With one of those lightning decisions that was the despair of his enemies and the envy of his friends, Simon Templar reorganised his offence. He wanted to talk to those two young men who had gone a-knocking at James Prather's door, but he didn't want them to know that he wanted to talk to them.

He looked gravely at Avalon.

"Will you do something for me?"

"I'll bake a cake or slice a throat," she said softly.
"Or cross Forty-second and Broadway against the traffic
light at Saturday noon."

"This is an even greater sacrifice," he said mockingly.
"I want you to go back into that apartment house and
do some lobby loitering."

Avalon didn't frown, didn't raise her eyebrows. She
meditated for the space of ten seconds. Then she raised
her eyes to his.

"I get the pitch, except for one thing. Who are you?"

"Your agent, of course."

"Of course. So I manage to be seen when they come
down, and will be here at the kerb with them when you
drive up. I'll be telling them I can't go with them, but
you'll allow me to be persuaded, provided you come
along. Then we all go off in your cab." She gave him a
quick kiss. "I should fall for a ten percenter yet. Everything happens to me."

She was out and clicking along the sidewalk on slim
heels. The Saint watched her for a moment and wondered. What a partner she would make! She had divined
his scheme of action, and with no prompting. She had
known, without words, what his plan was. All he had
had to do was sketch the bare outlines, and she had
filled in the details.

"Drive around the block," he told the driver.

It was on the third circumnavigation that the Saint
saw Avalon and the two seamen at the kerb in front of
the apartment house. He amused himself with the idea
that these were the only live persons he had seen on
his rounds : all others had been members of the Bronx
nobility walking their dogs.

"Stop there," he commanded, and the cab driver drew
up with a satisfying squeal of rubber.

been told you're more'n that. You see, I recognised you.
You've had too many photos printed in the papers—
Saint."

Simon smiled, a devil-may-care smile, a smile as light
as butterflies' worries.

"So? And now that we're putting everything on the
barrel-head, why are you holding that cannon on me?"

Avalon gasped, and glanced sidewise.

"Well," Sam Jeffries said, "I guess it ain't necessary.
I really wouldn't shoot you without'n you done more'n
you've did."

Simon grinned.

"Thanks. Just to get the record straight, I really am
this young lady's agent. She's a night-club singer."

Stocky Joe Hyman said: "Huh?"

Sam Jeffries made a threatening motion at his pal.

"'F she says she's a singer, she's a singer, see? 'N 'f
he says he's her agent, well, shaddup, see?"

"I didn't mean nothing," Joe said.

"Well, Mister?" Sam said to Simon.

The Saint eyed the gun, the neat blue suit, the maroon
tie, the long tanned face of Sam Jeffries. He began to
move one hand toward his inner coat pocket.

"May I smoke?"

"Sure," Sam said.

The Saint took out his cigarette case, that case which
had special properties that had before now helped him
out of tighter spots than this. Not that the case seemed
to differ from any similar case made of gold and
embellished with a tasteful amount of precious gems.
No, it seemed functional in design, if a bit on the ornate
side. And functional it was; for one of its edges could
be used as a razor. The toughest beard would fall before
that redoubtable keenness. Not only was it a weapon for

cutting bonds or throats, it contained ammunition which could be applied in sundry ways to the confusion of the Ungodly.

Interspersed among his regular brand were other special cigarettes which could blind, frighten, and fling into chaos such unsavoury members of the human race as the Saint wished to blind, frighten, or fling into chaotic action. Each of these explosive tubes consisted almost entirely of magnesium.

His sensitive fingers felt among the case's cargo to light upon a bona-fide smoke, which he lighted. He puffed a blue cloud at the ceiling and placed the case in a convenient jacket pocket. There might be use for it later. In doing so, he felt the outline of the small knife, Belle, which nestled in her case up his sleeve.

He eyed Sam Jeffries with that devilish carelessness that had made his name not only a by-word but a guide to independence.

"What do you mean, what now?"

"Well," Sam said, "I didn't recognise you at first. But after we was in the cab, see, I says, 'Sam, that's the Saint,' I says. And I asks myself what would the Saint want of the likes of us, and I gets no answer, see. So then I says to myself it'd be a good idea maybe if I didn't take no chances, so I hauls out my rod."

"Which fails to comfort me," the Saint murmured. His inaudible sigh of relief was let out carefully and imperceptibly. His mind was concerned with one beautiful thought. Sam Jeffries hadn't expected him to show up.

Avalon hadn't, then, tipped them off. If she were one of the Ungodly, she would have warned the two sailor boys. But she hadn't, and that made for singing in the veins.

He caught up his sudden joy in two mental hands and looked at it. It could be a treacherous kind of joy, going off half-cocked at the most stupid stimuli. Suppose she had warned Sam Jeffries. Would he be clever enough to put on an act of this sort? Perhaps not but perhaps yes, too. At any rate, Avalon might have been clever enough to instigate such an act.

So the whole situation solved nothing, as far as his estimate of Avalon was concerned. And it was becoming increasingly important that he arrive at a correct estimate of her intents and purposes.

For himself he had no fear. These were young men —boys, really, in experience—whom he could overpower, escape from or capture if he chose to do so. But if Avalon were in this with him, his actions might explode along a certain line; if she were not, they would certainly explode along other and more uncomfortable lines.

Not that the end result would be affected. The Saint felt that he was travelling along the right road. As soon as the sea came into the picture, he was convinced that at long last he was approaching the goal.

For he had mental visions of ships sailing out of New York harbour, through the Canals, Panama or Suez, heading west or east, but always with the Orient at one end of the run. Small ships, 3,000-ton freighters, carrying cargo to Calcutta; big ships, 20,000-ton liners of the restless deep, taking men and women to build a new world from the shattered remains.

And on these ships he saw men—boys from Glasgow, oldsters from the Bronx, trim officers from Liverpool— with an idea: "Benny sent me."

That Open Sesame formula of speak-easy days applied here, too. Benny sent me. The grilled door opened, you could libate at the bar, the house was yours. Every prospect pleased, and only the liquor was vile. Here, too, and now. Benny sent me. An agent passed over a parcel, it was stowed away, returned to New York and eventually to Benny.

Benny, in this case, being James Prather.

Maybe. In any case, it was vital to learn what these boys knew. What cares had they while sailing the seven (Seven? the Saint could think of nine, offhand) seas? What errands run, what messages carried? Were they unwitting or willing tools of—of whom?

That was the question.

And so the Saint said, in an effort to relax Sam Jeffries' upraised black brows and Joe Hyman's corrugated forehead: "Do you want to see my union card?"

This had not the desired effect on Joe's forehead, but Sam grinned sheepishly.

"That you're her agent? Naw, I guess not. Maybe I was a little quick on the draw, but I seen times when to be slow was to be too damned slow. Look, Mister, I'm sorry, I guess. What say we forget it?"

"Would you like to shake left-handed," Simon asked pleasantly, "or would you like to put away that postage stamp pistol?"

Sam dropped it into his jacket pocket, grinned anew, and gave Simon a hand that was hard as iron.

"Less just have fun, Saint."

"A pleasure, Sam."

Avalon went "Phew!" in an explosive release of tension. "Pardon my nerves," she said, "but these unorthodox introductions have a tendency to throw me."

Joe looked at everybody at once, a feat that did strange things to his round face.

"Ya mean this guy's d'Saint? Th' guy what diddles

cops an' crooks too, all to once? 'Zat who he is?"

Sam Jeffries gazed patiently at his shipmate.

"Look, we been talkin' for fifteen minutes about who he is, while we run up three bucks on the meter and'll wind up in the drink if we don't tell the guy where to go, so shaddup."

"I didn't mean nothin'," Joe murmured. "But hell's —hully criminy, I mean—the Saint!"

"So he's th' Saint, so what? Right now he's a guy goin' along to put a few belts away. Got any arguments?"

"Naw, but it's like—well, you know, well, hell, I mean——"

"Shaddup." To Avalon, Sam said: "Uh, Miss Dexter, we asked you to come along with us, 'n it seems to me this oughta be your party. Whyn't you tell th' helmsman where to throw out the anchor?"

Avalon looked at the Saint. He looked away. She turned to Joe, who was still wandering around in wonder at the Saint's being present.

"I'll go wherever Joe wants to go."

She was rewarded by one of the most complete smiles she had ever seen.

Not that Joe reminded you of a vaudeville comic hamming romantic embarrassment; there was no calculation in his pleasure. It was just that: pure pleasure. His round face took on a glow that made it like a lamp in a mine tunnel.

The Saint took his eyes away from the back window, through which he had been scrutinising traffic in their wake, and let them rest on Joe. Where would Joe want to go? The Stork? 21? Leon and Eddie's? Or some waterfront joint—Bill's Place, or some such.

It seemed that Joe was going to require some time to

decide. He was obviously accustomed to having decisions made for him: "Swab the deck," "Coil that rope,"
"Kick that guy in the kidneys." Here was responsibility,
and he wasn't quite ready for it. If Avalon had simply
told him to jump out of the cab window, there was no
doubt in the world that he would have done it. He
might have asked if she wanted him to do a jack-knife
or a belly-buster, but his final action would have been
to drape himself on the asphalt. But now there was a
choice concerned, he was so pleased at having his opinion
asked that the fact of the choice slipped his mind.

He sat grinning for so long that Sam jabbed him
with: "Well?"

Joe blinked. His grin faded slowly, like sky writing
in a gentle breeze.

"Huh? Oh. Well, gosh, I don't care."

The Saint was becoming very fond of Joe. Here was
a boy who would give out like a defective slot machine
if manipulated properly.

"She ast ya," Sam said patiently. "So you don't care.
We keep flitting around behind this meter till ya make
up ya mind? Name some place, any place!"

Joe blinked, and you could almost hear unused mental machinery begin to rattle and clank. The machinery
ground to a stop. His face once more was like a harvest
moon.

"Cookie's!" he cried, and was quiet.

The Saint suppressed a groan. He didn't like Cookie's
—Canteen or Cellar. He'd never visited the Canteen,
but his mind was made up.

On the other hand——

He considered the other hand. James Prather had
seen him and Avalon leave with Sam and Joe. That
fact would be reported, if the Saint's ideas on the situa-

tion were correct. Those receiving the report would in some way be tied up with Cookie's. Therefore, if they all turned up there in the late afternoon, before the crowd began to thicken, some overt action might be taken. Anything, he thought, to get this thing out in the open. Another point to be considered was Avalon. In the event of a fracas of any sort at Cookie's, she'd be more likely to declare her allegiance there than elsewhere.

"Splendid," the Saint said, and Avalon's half-formed answer died in her throat.

She might have been about to say all the obvious things: the place would be dull at this time of day, she didn't like it, it was a clip joint, haven of highgraders. But when the Saint spoke, she shot him a puzzled glance and was still.

Simon gave instructions to the driver, and they took off on a new tack.

"Why," Simon asked conversationally, "Cookie's?"

"All the guys," Sam Jeffries said, "keep tellin' ya if ya want a swell time, go there, if ya belong to th' Merchant Marine. Free drinks, free eats, maybe even a girl trun in. Jo here believes everything anybody tells 'im."

"Sometimes," Joe said, with the air of a great philosopher, "it turns out that way."

"Yeh!" Sam snorted. "Remember in Kobe how that——"

"Aw, that," Joe broke in. "He was ribbin' us."

Simon slipped in smoothly and took the conversation over. "How is the Orient?"

"Still shot to hell," Sam said. "Gonna be a long time before all them buildings go up again."

"Did you hear about Cookie's, even there?"

"Yeah, you know, guys on other ships."

"And you've never been to Cookie's before?"

"No."

"Where did you go on this last trip?"

While Sam launched a graphic account of their travels, Simon considered the fact that neither of these boys had been to Cookie's before. This seemed hardly in keeping with the pattern which Simon had begun to put together in his mind. He felt that the link must be somewhere between ships darting about the sea and Cookie's Cellar. James Prather?

Or the late lamented Gamaliel Bradford Foley?

Foley had been tied up with Dr. Zellermann. Dr. Zellermann with Cookie's, or some members of Cookie's entourage. Therefore a link existed somewhere.

Anyway, here they were. Simon paid off the taxi, and they went inside. The place was almost deserted, but a few people were around.

Among these was James Prather, talking to Kay Natello. Prather looked up at the party's entrance, narrowed his eyes and walked toward them.

CHAPTER THREE

How Mr. Prather said Little, and Dr. Zellermann said Even Less

THE Saint had never considered himself to be psychic. He had learned that by adding the factors of a situation he could forecast the probable moment when Death would leer at him over a gunsight, or ride the business end of a club, or sing through the air on the point of a knife. He had learned that, when he subconsciously placed such factors in their proper alignment and came up with a subconscious answer, his adrenal glands went quickly into action with a suddenness that brought a tingling to the back of his neck and the tips of his fingers.

He did not regard this sensation as the result of a psychic gander into the immediate future, nor as the brushing of the back of his neck by an ectoplasmic hand once belonging to the goose-over-a-grave school of pre-monitory shuddering. The tingle he felt when James Prather followed his bulging eyes across the deserted floor of Cookie's Cellar was, he knew, the result of his adrenals sitting up and taking notice.

For Simon had added the factors, and their sum total was danger. Not that he expected explosive action at the moment. He could have written the dialogue to come almost word for word. These characters weren't certain where and how the Saint fitted into the picture. Their motivation at the moment was the desire for such knowledge, and they would go about satisfying that desire in a fashion designed to be subtle and off-hand.

Nobody would say, yet: "Just what the hell are you doing here?"

The Saint said under his breath to Avalon: "Get a table. Yonder bucko would have words with me. I'll join you."

She sandwiched herself between Sam and Joe and piloted them to the far wall, which had been pleasantly blank before Ferdinand Pairfield had agonised upon it in pastel, and the Saint waited for Prather.

"Just what the hell are you doing here?" Prather demanded.

The Saint did not allow so much as the quiver of an

eyelash to acknowledge his downfall as a prophet. His lazy smile and mocking blue eyes only indicated amusement at the gauche approach. Prather flushed under the steady gaze, and his lobster-like eyes shifted away and back. In their shifting away, they touched on Joe Hyman and Sam Jeffries but showed no trace of recognition.

"Comrade," the Saint said, "far back in the history of this country certain gentlemen flung powder and shot about in the cause of freedom. Such points as they have been traditionally passed down through the years, and one of these points is the untrammelled right to visit such places as this, with its steel-trap economy, its bad air and worse drinks. Just why anyone in his right mind should like to exercise his right to such dubious pleasure is beyond me, but there it is."

"There's something fishy about this," Prather said in a sort of bewildered whine. "First, you come to my place with a song and dance about research. Then you follow me here. Why? I know who you are. You're the Saint. But I can't see why you followed me."

"Follow you? Dear boy, I wouldn't follow you into the flossiest bagnio this side of Paradise. But now that you seem to have made such a lightning trip here, I'm happy to see you. Won't you join my party? I'm still gathering material."

Prather regarded the table where Avalon parried verbs with Sam Jeffries with the concentration of a man sucking a piece of popcorn out of a cavity.

"Thank you," he said with a grimness that was rather surprising. "I'll be glad to."

Sam was on his life story, apparently having begun at the present, and was working backward.

" . . . and there was this guy we had to see in Shanghai. Joe wanted to get drunk right off, but I says no, we gotta see this guy before . . ."

He broke off, looked up. No flicker of recognition moved his brown face as he glanced incuriously at Prather. To the Saint, Sam said: "I was just tellin' Miss Dexter about our last trip."

Something happened, but the Saint didn't catch it. It could have been a glance, a shake of the head, a kick in the ankle, from James Prather. For Sam suddenly froze. He didn't look at Prather, he didn't look at anybody, but you could see his thoughts and amiable chatter roll themselves up like armadillos and become impregnable and lifeless. All the warm lights went out of his eyes, and his smile became a fixed liability.

His social immobility somehow conveyed itself to Joe, who underwent little change to achieve Sam's frozen state. Both young men rose to shake hands as the Saint performed introductions, but, like Mudville on the night of Casey's disaster, there was no joy in them. Sam remained standing, long, lean, and brown.

"Guess we better shove off, huh, Joe?"

"Yeah," Joe said, meeting nobody's eye. "Guess so."

"Don't run away, boys," Avalon said. But she said it perfunctorily. She knew they were going. Her tone was a politeness, not an urging.

"When the party's just starting?" said the Saint. He, too, knew they were going. A kick, a frown, a shake of the head. These had made the boys jittery.

"Well, Saint," Sam said. "You know how it is. Just back from a long trip. We were kinda thinkin' of girls of our own. Course, I'll have to get one for Joe, here, but still——" He nodded at Avalon. "Thought we had something there—uh, Miss. But seems she's staked out. So we'll blow."

More handshakes, and they were gone.

Kay Natello came over to greet them, and in that voice like a nutmeg grater on tin cans asked, "What'll it be?"

She didn't seem to be anxious to cut up old touchés with Simon, so he played it her way.

"Old Foresters all around. Doubles," he added, remembering the strength of drinks at Cookie's.

"Now," the Saint said when Kay had gone. "Tell me about Dr. Zellermann.

"What is there to tell?"

Prather didn't seem uncomfortable. There was, in his mind, nothing to tell. At least, he gave that impression.

"He's a psychiatrist," he went on. "A good one, maybe. Any rate, he gets good prices."

"Well," the Saint said. "Maybe we'd better drop him. Let's just have fun, kids."

Avalon looked several volumes of unprintable material at the Saint and asked: "How do you propose to do that?"

"By displaying my erudition, darling." The Saint smiled gently at her, and then bent attentive eyes on Prather as he said: "For instance. Do you know the word 'cougak'?"

This brought no response. Simon sighed inwardly. Might as well get it out into the open, he thought. "It's the term applied to the bloom of a certain plant known as *Pavarer somniferum*. It's cultivated chiefly in Asia. After the poppy flowers, and the leaves fall off, the remaining pod develops a bloom, easily rubbed off with the fingers, called cougak. Then it is time to make the incision."

"What are you talking about?" Avalon demanded.

"Mr. Prather, I think," said the Saint.

Prather blinked his overblue eyes at Simon.

"I'm sorry, but I don't know what you mean."

"It really doesn't matter," the Saint said. "Let's talk about something else."

He noted that Kay Natello, who had been hovering in the middle distance, took her departure at this point and vanished through the archway at the back. Had there been a signal? If so, he hadn't caught it.

"Mr. Prather," he said, "you must find life quite exhilarating. Contact with the major ports of the world, and all that."

Prather stared, his eyes more lobster-like than usual.

"What are you talking about?"

There was no mistaking the honest bewilderment in the prominent blue eyes, and this gave the Saint pause. According to his ideas on the organisation he was bucking, Prather would be one of the key men. Sam Jeffries had substantiated this notion, in his interrupted story to Avalon: " . . . and there was this guy we had to see in Shanghai."

That fitted in with the whole theory of "Benny sent me." A contract was made here, instructions given, perhaps an advance made. Then the delivery of a package in the Orient or the Near East, which was returned to New York and duly turned over to James Prather or a prototype. All this made sense, made a pattern.

But here was James Prather, obviously bewildered by the plainest kind of a lead. Was the man cleverer than he seemed? Was he putting on an act that could mislead that expert act-detector, the Saint? Or was he honestly in the dark about the Saint's meaning? And if he was, why was he here immediately after a visit from two sailors freshly back from the Orient?

Mr. James Prather, it seemed, was in this picture somewhere, and it behoved the Saint to find out where.

"Well," Simon said, "no matter. We have more important things to do, such as demolishing our—— But we have no drinks." He motioned to an aproned individual, who came to the table and assumed an attitude of servility. "Three more of the same. Old Forester."

The waiter took the empty glasses and went away. The Saint turned his most winning smile on Prather.

"I wasn't really shooting in the dark," he said. "But I guess my remarks weren't down the right alley."

"Whatever you say," Prather replied, "I like. You have a good quality of voice. Though I don't see why you should spend any time with me."

"Remember?" Simon asked. "I'm still doing research on Dr. Zellermann."

Prather laughed. "I'd forgotten. Ah, here come our drinks."

The waiter, an individual, like the village blacksmith, with brawny arms, came across the empty dance floor with a tray flattened on one upturned palm. It was obvious to the Saint's practised eye that the man's whole mental attitude had changed. He had gone away trailing a fretful desire to please; he approached with newfound independence.

He was a stocky individual, broad of shoulder, lean of hip, heavy in the legs. His face was an eccentric oval, bejewelled with small turquoise eyes, crowned with an imposing nose that overhung a mouth of rather magnificent proportions. His chin was a thing of angles, on which you could hang a lantern.

But the principal factor in his changed aspect was his independence. He carried the tray of drinks as though the nearest thing to his heart was the oppor-

tunity and reason to toss them into the face of a customer. Not only that, but each of the three glasses was
that type known as "Old Fashioned."

Each glass was short, wide of mouth, broad of base.
And in each drink was a slice of orange and a cherry
impaled on a toothpick.

"Sorry," said the Saint as the waiter distributed the
glasses, "but I ordered highballs, not Old Fashioneds."

"Yeh?" said the waiter. "You trying to make
trouble?"

"No. I'm merely trying to get a drink."

"Well, ya act like to me you're tryin' to make trouble.
Ya order Old Fashioneds, 'n then ya yell about highballs. What's comin' off here?"

"Nothing," Simon said patiently, "is coming off here.
I'm simply trying to get what I ordered."

"Ya realise I'll hafta pay for this, don't ya?" the
waiter demanded.

"I'll pay for them," Simon said in the same gentle
voice. "If you made a mistake, it won't cost you
anything. Just bring us three Old Foresters—highballs."

"And what's gonna happen to these drinks?"

"That," the Saint said, "I don't know. You may rub
them into the bar-tender's hair, for all of me."

The waiter lifted his lip.

"Lissen, the bar-tender's my brother-in-law."

The Saint's lips tightened.

"Then rub them into his back. Will you get our
drinks?"

The waiter stared sullenly for a moment.

"Well, all right. But no more cracks about my
brother-in-law, see?"

He went away. The Saint watched him for a moment,

decided against any action. His attention drifted from the waiter to the Pairfield murals.

"It's an odd mind," he remarked, "that can contrive such unattractive innovations in the female form divine." He indicated a large sprawling figure on the far wall. "Take Gertie over there. Even if her hips did have Alemite lubrication points all over them, is it quite fair to let the whole world in on her secret?"

"What I like," Avalon said, "is the hedge for hair. That pent-house effect throws me."

"I'm sorry," James Prather said, "but I feel a little uncomfortable looking at those designs. This one over here, with each lock of hair ending in a hangman's knot. I——"

He broke off, with an ineffectual gesture with his pale hands.

"The poor man's Dali," murmured the Saint. "Here come our—what *are* those drinks?"

They were pale green, in tall flared glasses, each with a twist of lime peel floating near the top.

The Saint repeated his question to the sullen waiter.

"Lissen," that character said. "I got no time to be runnin' back and forth for you. These here are Queen Georgianas, 'n if you don't want 'em, rub 'em in your——" He glanced at Avalon, coloured. "—Well, rub 'em."

"But I ordered," the Saint said very patiently, "Old Foresters. Highballs."

"'N if you're gonna be fussy," the waiter said, "you're lucky to get anything. Wait a minute. Here comes the manager."

The manager was thin, dapper, and dark, like George Raft in his halcyon days. He strode up to the table, took in the situation with an expressionless look of his dark eyes, and turned them on the Saint.

"Yes?" he said.

"Whom do you have to know here?" Simon inquired. "I've been trying to get some *bourbon* for about thirty minutes."

"Why don't you ask for it then?" suggested the manager.

"Look," Simon said. "I don't mind buying your watered drinks at about three times the normal prices. All I want is the right flavour in the water. I do not want Queen Georgianas, or Old Fashioneds. I want Old Forester. It's a simple thing. All the waiter does is remember the order until he gets back to the bar. I'll write it out for him if he has a defective memory."

"Nothin's wrong with my memory," the waiter growled. "Maybe you'd like these drinks in your puss, smart guy. You asked for Queen Georgianas, and you're gonna take 'em."

Simon clenched his hands under the rim of the table.

"Believe me," he said earnestly, "the last desire I have is to cause difficulty. If I must take these obscenities, I'll take them. But will you please, please get us a round of bourbon highballs?"

"Why don't you go away, if the service doesn't please you?" asked the George Raft manager.

"The service," the Saint said, "leaves nothing to be desired, except everything."

"Then why don't you just go away?" asked the manager.

The Saint decided to be stubborn.

"Why?"

"No reason," the manager said. "We reserve the right to refuse service to anyone. Our sign says so."

He indicated a sign above the bar.

"And you are refusing me service?"

"No. Not if you don't cause trouble."

"And?"

The manager nodded to the waiter. "Get him his drinks."

"I'm not gonna serve him," the waiter said.

The manager stamped a gleaming shoe. "Did you hear me?"

The waiter went away.

"Now," the Saint said, "where were we? Oh, yes, we were discussing," he said to the manager, "the more obscure aspects of suicide in American night clubs. Would you have anything to add to our data soon?"

The manager smiled a crooked smile and departed. The Saint caught the eye of James Prather, and formed a question: "Now that we've gone through the preliminary moves, shall we get down to business?"

Prather goggled rather like a fish in an aquarium tank, but before the Saint could begin to explain he caught sight of the waiter returning with a tray of pink concoctions in champagne glasses.

"I," Simon announced, "am beginning to become annoyed. *Avec* knobs on."

The waiter slammed the tray on the table and distributed the drinks. The Saint eyed his.

It was definitely not a Pink Lady. Nor was it pink champagne. There was grenadine in it, judging from the viscosity apparent to the eye. There might be gin, or even water. He raised his eyes.

"What—is—this?"

The waiter's eyes were like small blue marbles. "They bourbon and sodas, see?"

"Pink bourbon?"

"Ja ever see any other kind?" the waiter snarled.

"I believe," Simon said gently, "that I have been patient. Compared to the way I've conducted myself, burros are subjects for strait-jackets. You have brought four rounds of liquid abortions that no self-respecting canned-heat hound would dip a finger in. While this went on I have kept my temper. Job himself would stack up beside me like a nervous cat. I have taken all your insults with a smile. But I warn you, if you don't bring the right order on your next trip, you are going to wish your mother had spanked the bad manners out of you before I had to."

"So you wanta make trouble, huh?" The waiter signalled. "Hey, Jake!"

The bar-tender, who seemed to be Jake, stopped shaking a whisky sour at the top of the motion, looking something like a circus giant caught in a ballet pose. He was pushing six feet and a half with shoulders perhaps not so wide as a door, but wide enough. He had a face like the butt end of a redwood log, and hands like great brown clamps on the shaker.

His customers turned to regard the tableau across the big room according to the stages of inebriety they'd reached. A middle-aged man with a brief moustache twirled it at Avalon. A lady of uncertain balance lifted one side of a bright mouth at the Saint. A young couple stared, and turned back to their private discussion, which, to judge from their expression, was going to wind up in the nearest bedroom.

Jake then set down the shaker, and walked around the end of the bar. At the same moment a third man, large and aproned, came out of the archway and joined him. They marched together across the dance floor, side by side, and advanced upon the Saint. It was obvious that he was their objective.

The Saint didn't move. He watched the approach of the brawny gents with the bright-eyed interest of a small boy at his first circus. He noted the width of Jake's shoulders, the practised walk bespeaking sessions in a prize-ring, and the shamble of his companion. He weighed them, mentally, and calculated the swiftness of their reflexes. He smiled.

He could see Avalon's clenched fists, just below the rim of the table, and from the corner of his eye he noted Prather's bug-eyed interest.

Jake directed a calm, steady, brown-eyed gaze at Simon Templar.

"Get out of here. Now."

Simon didn't seem to push his chair back. He seemed only to come to an astonished attention. But in that straightening motion, his chair was somehow a good three inches back from the edge of the table and he could come to his feet without being hampered.

"Yes?" he drawled with hopeful interest. "How jolly. Ask your boss to come out and explain."

"The boss don't need to explain," said the spokes-man. "We'll do all the explainin' necessary."

"Then suppose you do, my lad."

"What is this all about, Jake?" Avalon asked.

"The boss don't want him here, that's all. And we'll throw him out if he don't scram." Jake turned back to the Saint. "Look, chum, we ain't anxious to spread your pretty face all around like gravy. But we can, and will, if'n you don't beat it. And don't come back."

The Saint gestured at the table.

"You can see I haven't finished my drink. Nor has my lady friend."

"She can stay. It's just you that's goin'."

The Saint smiled mockingly. "It is always a mystery to me how human beings can become so misguided as to assume impossibilities. I should think anybody would know I'm not going out of here without Miss Dexter. She has an inflexible rule; namely, 'I'm gonna leave with the guy what brung me.' Namely, yours truly."

"Can the gab," Jake said. "You goin' out on your feet, or would you rather pick up teeth as you crawl out?"

Jake didn't seem to be angry, or impatient. He was merely giving the Saint a choice. Like: do you want your nails filed round or pointed?

Simon got lazily to his feet.

"Sorry, Mr. Prather," he said. "I was just getting interested in our conversation. Be with you in a moment. The children, you know. They get annoying at times and have to be cut back to size. . . . Jake, you shouldn't be such a naughty boy, really you shouldn't. Papa's told you before about interrupting your elders. Run along and play now, and you won't be chastised."

Jake nodded at his cohorts, and they moved at once. The Saint's first lightning move was to remove one from the fray with a short right jab that travelled no more than three inches but carried 180 pounds of muscled steel in motion behind it. The aproned bruiser folded his bulk against the wall between the widespread feet of one of Ferdinand Pairfield's figures and sat there with a vacuous mouth and eyes which, had they been stained, could have served as church windows.

In this move, however, Simon's attention was distracted for the fraction of a second from Jake, and that was enough. Jake made a flying leap over one corner of the table and clasped the Saint around his waist with a fervour that would have reduced Jake's girl friend to panting acquiescence.

This threw the Saint slightly off balance, and the waiter tried to take advantage of this by kicking Simon in the groin.

The Saint twisted, caught the man's ankle with his free hand, wrenched his other hand loose and began to unscrew the man's leg from the knee joint. Several welkins split asunder as the victim howled like a wounded wolf. Presently, within the space of time required to bat an eye, there was a most satisfying crack as the leg came unjointed at the hip, and the Saint turned his full attention to the leech-like Jake.

He went about that worthy's demolishment with a detached and unhurried calm. A left to the chin to straighten him up, a right to the stomach to bend him in the middle, another left, another right, and Jake gave the appearance of a polite man with the stomach ache bowing to a friend.

One devastating right to the button, and Jake slid across the stamp-sized dance floor on his back. He came to a gentle stop and lay gazing empty-eyed at the ceiling.

Sounds came from the back, sounds indicating a gathering of fresh forces. The Saint turned to Avalon.

"Shall we go, darling?" he drawled.

2

Which was all highly entertaining, not to say invigorating and healthful, Simon reflected later; but it added very little progress toward the main objective.

Certainly he had been given evidence that his attention was unwelcome to sundry members of the Ungodly; but that was hardly a novel phenomenon in his

interfering life. Once the Saint had exhibited any definite interest in their affairs and had been identified, the
Ungodly could invariably be relied on to experience
some misgivings, which might lead rather logically to
mayhem. Certainly the proffered mayhem had recoiled,
as it usually did, upon the initiators, who would doubtless approach this form of exercise more circumspectly
next time; but that could hardly be called progress. It
just meant that the Saint himself would have to be
more careful.

He had failed to learn any more about Mr. Prather's
precise place in the picture, or the relationship of the
other characters who flitted in and out of the convolutions of the impalpable organisation which he was
trying to unravel—or, for that matter, about Avalon's
real place in the whole crooked cosmogony.

Simon forced himself ruthlessly to remember that.
. . . With all their intimacy, their swift and complete
companionship, he still knew nothing. Nothing but
what he felt; and better men than he had come to disaster from not drawing the distinction between belief
and knowledge. The Saint had many vanities, but one
of them had never been the arrogant confidence that
sometime, somewhere, there could not be among the
ranks of the Ungodly a man or a woman who would
have the ability to make a sucker out of him. He had
waited for that all his life; and he was still waiting,
with the same cold and tormenting vigilance.

And yet, when he called Avalon the next morning,
there was nothing cold in his mind when her voice
answered.

"Good morning," he said.

"Good morning, darling," she said, and her voice
woke up with it. "How are you to-day?"

"Excited."

"What about?"

"Because I've got a date for lunch."

"Oh." The voice died again.

He laughed.

"With a beautiful girl . . . named Avalon."

"Oh." Such a different inflexion. As if the sun came out again. "You're a beast. I've a good mind not to be there."

"There are arguments against it," he admitted. "For one thing, we can't be alone."

"You mean the restaurant has to let other people in? We could fix that. Come over here, and I'll make an omelette."

"I'd like that much better. But it wouldn't work. I've still got a date. And you're going to keep it with me. We're having lunch with Zellermann."

"Did you call him?"

"He called me again, and I didn't see how I could get out of it. As a matter of fact, I decided I didn't want to. So much persistence is starting to intrigue me. And I do want to know more about him. And I don't think he can do much to me in 21."

"Is that where we're going?"

"Yes. I'll pick you up at twelve o'clock."

"I'll put on my silliest hat."

"If you do," said the Saint, "I'll be called away in the middle of lunch and leave you with him."

They were on time to the minute, but when Simon asked for the table he was told that Zellermann was already waiting for them.

The doctor stood up as they threaded a way between tables to his. Simon noted with some satisfaction that Zellermann's lips were still considerably swollen, although the fact would not have been so obvious to anyone who was not acquainted with the medicine man's mouth in its normal state.

He looked very much the Park Avenue psychiatrist —tall, leonine, carelessly but faultlessly dressed, with one of those fat smiles that somehow reminded the Saint of fresh shrimps.

"My dear Mr. Templar. And Miss Dexter. So glad you could manage the time. Won't you sit down?"

They did, and he did.

Dr. Zellermann displayed as much charm as a bee tree has honey.

"Miss Dexter, I feel that I must apologise for the other night. I am inclined to forget that universal adjustment to my psychological patterns has not yet been made."

"Don't let it worry you," Avalon said. "You paid for it."

A slight flush tinted the doctor's face as he looked at the Saint.

"My apologies to you, too, sir."

Simon grinned. "I didn't feel a thing."

Dr. Zellermann flushed deeper, then smiled.

"But that's all forgotten. We can be friendly together, and have a pleasant lunch. I like to eat here. The cuisine is excellent, the service——"

There was more of this. Considerably more. The Saint let his eyes rove over the dining-room which clattered discreetly with glass and silverware. Waiters went unobtrusively from table to table. Those with trays held the Saint's eyes.

Dr. Zellermann finished his eulogy of the restaurant, followed Simon's gaze.

"Oh, a drink, a drink by all means. Waiter!"

The waiter, so completely different from those sampled by the Saint in Cookie's the day before, came to their table as if he had crawled four miles over broken glass.

"May I serve you, sir?"

"Martinis, Manhattans?" the doctor inquired.

The Saint and Avalon ordered double Manhattans, the doctor a Martini, and the waiter genuflected away.

"So nice of you to invite us," the Saint said across the table. "A free lunch, as my drunken uncle used to say, is a free lunch."

Dr. Zellermann smiled.

"I somehow feel that you haven't quite had your share of free lunches, Mr. Templar. I feel that you have quite a few coming to you."

"Ah?" Simon queried.

He looked at Avalon immediately after he'd tossed the monosyllabic interrogation at the doctor. She sat quietly, with her gold-brown hair immaculate, her brown eyes wide, her small but definite chin pushed forward in a questing motion. At that moment, the Saint would have wagered anything he ever hoped to have that this green-clad, trim, slim, smartly turned out girl knew nothing about the problem that was taking up most of his time.

"In my work as a psychiatrist," the snowy-maned doctor explained, "I have learned a number of things. One of the main factors I take into consideration in the evaluation of a personality is whether that person is behind in the receipt of rewards. Each individual, as far as I have been able to discover, has put more into life than he ever gets out."

"Not according to what I was taught," Avalon said. "You get what you pay for. You get out of life, or a job, or a pail, or any damned thing, what you put into it, and no more. Otherwise, it's perpetual motion."

"Ah, no," Dr. Zellermann said. "If that were true, the sum total of all human effort would produce energies equal only to the sum total of all human effort. That would make change impossible. Yet we progress. The human race lives better, eats better, drinks better, each year. This indicates something. Those who are trying to cause the race to better itself—and they are less than the sum total of human beings, if not a minority —*must* be putting in more than they ever get out. If the law of equatorial returns is true, then it is quite obvious that a number of persons are dying before their time."

"I don't get you," Avalon said.

"Let's put it simply," the doctor replied. He broke off for the waiter to distribute their drinks. "If the energy you expend on living gives you only that amount of life, then your living conditions will never improve. Correct?"

"Umm."

"But your living conditions do improve. You have more and better food than your great-great-grandmother, or your grandfather thirty-eight times removed. Much better. Somebody, therefore, has put more into life than he has taken out, as long as the general living level of the human race continues to improve."

"And so?"

"And so," Dr. Zellermann said, "if the theory that we get no more out of life than we put into it is true, somebody is in the red. A lot of somebodies. Because the human race keeps progressing. And if each individual got no more out of what he put into it, life on the whole would remain the way it is."

"Umm."

"Are ideas energy?" the Saint asked.

"There you have it," Dr. Zellermann said. "Are ideas energy." It wasn't a question. "Are they? I don't know. A certain amount of energy must go into the process of producing ideas which may be translated into practical benefits to the race. What that amount of energy is, or whether it can be measured, is a point to be discussed in future years by scientists who are equipped with instruments we have never heard of."

"But have we heard of the Orient?" asked the Saint.

"I don't follow you," Dr. Zellermann said.

Simon paused while their drinks were delivered; and while he waited it crossed his mind that the trouble with all the creeps he had met so far in this business was that they responded to a leading question about as actively as a dead mouse would to a slab of Camembert. It also crossed his mind that a great deal of aimless chatter was being cast upon the chaste air of that burnished beanery.

Was there some dark and undefined purpose in the doctor's Hegelian calisthenics? Did that turgid bouillabaisse of unsemantic verbiage have significance, or was it only stalling for time? Surely the distinguished salver of psyches hadn't asked Simon and Avalon here to philosophise with them?

Well, the ulterior motives, if any, would be revealed in due course. Meanwhile, it seemed as if the vocal merry-go-round, if it had to keep rolling, could spin to more profitable purpose.

So Simon Templar, in that completely unexpected fashion of his which could be so disconnecting, turned the channels of the conversation toward another direction of his own choosing.

"In the Orient," he said, "the standard of living remains a fairly deplorable constant. Millions of those people put an astounding amount of energy into the process of survival, and what do they get?" His shrug answered the question.

Dr. Zellermann made a small motion with one hand. He took his fingers from the stem of his Martini glass and moved them. The Saint, who happened to be looking at the hand, marvelled that so much could be expressed in a gesture. The small, graceful, yet definite motion said as clearly as if the thought were expressed in boxcar letters: "But, my dear Mr. Templar!"

"What do they get?" Dr. Zellermann asked, looking somewhat like an equine bishop granting an indulgence. He answered his own question. "Life, my dear Mr. Templar—the only actually free gift in the universe. What they do with it is not only their business, but the end product is not open to censure or sympathy."

"Still the old free-will enthusiast?"

"That's all we have. What we do with it is our own fault."

"I can be president, eh, or dog catcher?"

"That's up to you," Zellermann said.

"A moment, old boy. Suppose we consider Chang."

The doctor's eyebrows said: "Chang?"

"As a guinea-pig," the Saint explained. "Chang, once upon a time, chanced to smoke a pipe of opium. It was free, and anything for a laugh, that's our Chang. Then he had another pipe, later. And another. Not free, now. Oh, no. There are dealers who have to make a living; and behind the dealers there are interested governments. So Chang becomes an addict. He lets his family, his home, everything, go hang. Where is the free will,

Doctor, when he's driven by that really insatiable desire?"

"It was his decision to smoke the first pipe."

"Not entirely," the Saint pointed out. "Someone was interested in making it available. You can't tell me that it wouldn't be possible to restrict the production of opium to established medical requirements if the principal world governments were really interested. Yet India alone produces more opium than the whole world could use legitimately. Very profitable. So profitable that governments have come out fighting to keep the market open. Do you happen to remember the so-called Boxer Rebellion?"

"Vaguely," Zellermann said in bored tones.

"All the wretched Chinese wanted was their own country back," said the Saint. "But the—ah, Powers, made a great pitch about rescuing their missionaries, and so put down the rebellion and so saved the market."

"Isn't this rather *non sequitur*?" asked the doctor.

"Is it?" Simon asked. "If you're tired of Chang, throw him away—in his millions. He means no more personally than a treeful of yaks, because we have no contact with his daily so-called living. But take Joe Doakes in Brooklyn."

"Really, Mr. Templar, your train of thought is confusing."

"It shouldn't be, dear boy. Just translate Chang into Joe, and consider the identical operation in New York. Even America the Beautiful, let us face it, contains certain citizens who don't much care how they make a million dollars so long as they make it. And particularly don't care who gets hurt in the process. So now Joe's the boy we're after. He's like Chang, in the low income group, not averse to a bit of petty thievery, possibly ready for a pipe after a hard day's pocket-picking."

"Who," Zellermann inquired, "are 'we'?"

"We here at the table," the Saint said expansively, "for purposes of hypothetical discussion."

"Not me," Avalon interpolated. "I got troubles of my own, without including pipes."

"Let's say you are 'we,' Doctor. Your problem is two-fold. You must transport the stuff, and then sell it. If you solve the transportation problem, you have to find Joe. The first problem is fairly elemental. Who goes to the Orient these days? Sailors. They can bring in the stuff. Finding Joe is easy, too. Go into the nearest pool hall and turn to your right."

"This leads us where, Mr. Templar?" Dr. Zellermann asked. "Though I admit your conversation has its scintillating aspects, I fail to see——" He let it hang.

"To this point, comrade. A group of men putting drugs into the hands—mouths—of persons rendered irresponsible by economic circumstance are creating tools. Governments learned that a long time ago. Beat a man down enough, and he'll come to think that's the normal way to be. But private groups—shall we say rings—who are foolish enough to think they can get away with it couldn't be expected to do anything but follow an established lead."

The Saint watched for any reaction from the doctor. He would have settled for a tapping finger, but the Park Avenue psychiatrist would have made the Great Stone Face look like Danny Kaye.

Simon shrugged.

He looked at Avalon and winked.

"In other words, your theory—'*Faites ce que voudras,*' if I may borrow from an older philosopher—is jake so long as you and I are the guys who are doing what they damn please. So far I only know one of your forms of self-indulgence, and you only know one of mine. I have others."

Avalon smiled; and the Saint marvelled that all those people who were so busy clattering their silverware, churning the air with inanities, and trying to impress a lot of people who were only interested in impressing them, shouldn't feel the radiance of that smile and halt in the middle of whatever they were doing. They should feel that smile, and pause. And think of things lost, of beauties remembered, and recapture rapture again.

But they didn't. The bebosomed Helen Hokinson woman at the nearest table giggled at the young man opposite her; the promoter type over there went right on citing figures, no doubt, blowing a bugle of prosperity; the Hollywood actress went on ogling the Broadway producer, who went on ogling her, being just as happy to get her in his highly speculative play as she was to have the chance of reviving a career which had failed to quite keep up with her press agent.

The Saint sighed.

He turned his attention back to Dr. Zellermann, waiting for a hint of the point that must be shown sometime.

"Another drink?" asked the doctor.

They had another drink; and then Zellermann said, with a thread of connection which was so strained that it sang: "I imagine one of the things you would like is forming theories about current crimes as the newspapers report them. That Foley murder in Brooklyn, for instance, rather intrigues me."

The Saint took a deep pull on his cigarette; and a little pulse began to beat way inside him as he realised that this, at last, whatever it was, was it.

His own decision was made in a split second. If that was how Zellermann wanted it, okay. And if Zellermann favoured the shock technique, Simon was ready to bounce it right back without batting an eyelid and see what happened.

"Yes," he said, "even in these days of flowing lucre, it must be sad to lose a good patient."

"I wasn't thinking of the money," Dr. Zellermann began. He broke off suddenly, leaving the remainder of the thought unexpressed. "How did you know he was a patient of mine?"

The Saint sipped at his Manhattan.

"I saw his name on your secretary's appointment pad," he said calmly.

"But look here, Templar. When were you in my office?"

"Oh, I thought you knew," Simon said with a touch of surprise. "I broke in on Thursday night."

3

This brought motionless silence to Dr. Zellermann. He eyed the Saint coldly for a long moment. Then he said: "Are you in the habit of breaking and entering?"

"I wouldn't say it's a habit, old boy. The word habit has connotations of dullness. As a matter of fact, I should say I have no habits whatever, as such, unless you classify breathing as a habit. That is one to which I cling with—on occasion—an almost psychotic firmness. There have been times, I admit, when certain persons, now among the dear departed, have tried to persuade me to give up breathing. I am glad to say that their wiles had no effect on my determination."

The doctor shook his head irritably.

"You know you committed a felony?"

"By going on breathing?"

Dr. Zellermann raised his voice slightly. "By breaking into my office."

"Technically, I suppose I did," Simon confessed. "But I was sure you'd understand. After all, I was only applying your own pet philosophy. I felt like doing it, so I did."

"As the victim," Zellermann said, "I'm surely entitled to hear your reason."

The Saint grinned.

"Like the bear that came over the mountain, to see what I could see. Very interesting it was, too. Did Ferdinand Pairfield do your decorating?"

Dr. Zellermann's face was impassive.

"A philosophy, Mr. Templar, is one thing. Until the world adopts that philosophy, the law is something else. And under the present laws you are guilty of a crime."

"Aren't you sort of rubbing it in a bit, Ernst?" Simon protested mildly.

"Only to be sure that you understand your position."

"All right then. So I committed a crime. I burgled your office. For that matter, I burgled the late Mr. Foley's apartment too—and his murder intrigues me just as much as you. So what?"

Dr. Zellermann turned his head and glanced across the room. He made an imperious gesture with a crooking finger.

The Saint followed his gaze and saw two men in inconspicuous blue suits at a far table detach themselves from the handles of coffee cups. One of them pushed something small and black under the table. Both rose and came toward Dr. Zellermann's table. They had that deadpan, slightly bored expression which has be-

come an occupational characteristic of plain-clothes'
men.

There was no need for them to show their badges to
convince the Saint, but they did.

"You heard everything?" Dr. Zellermann asked.

The shorter of the two, who had a diagonal scar on
his square chin, nodded.

Simon ducked his head and looked under the table.
He saw a small microphone from which a wire ran
down the inside of one of the legs of the table and
disappeared under the rug. The Saint straightened and
wagged an admiring head.

"That, my dear doctor, is most amusing. Here I
thought that I was talking privately, and it would be
your word against mine in any consequent legal name-
calling. It simply didn't occur to me that you'd—er—
holler copper."

Dr. Zellermann paid no attention to Simon. He spoke
to Scar-chin.

"You know this man is the Saint, a notorious crimi-
nal, wanted in various parts of the world for such things
as murder, blackmail, kidnapping, and so forth?"

"Not wanted for, chum," the Saint corrected him
amiably. "Merely suspected of."

Scar-chin looked at his partner, a man with sad
spaniel eyes. "Guess we better go."

Spaniel Eyes laid a hand on the Saint's arm.

"One moment," Simon said. This was said quietly,
but there was the sound of bugles in the command.
Spaniel Eyes withdrew his arm. The Saint looked at
Zellermann. "Your information came from somewhere.
You didn't deduce this by yourself and so lay a trap.
Did Avalon tip you off?"

"Oh, Simon!" she cried. "No, darling, no!"

Her voice was brimming with anguish and outrage. Real or simulated, the Saint couldn't tell. He didn't look at her. He held the doctor's eyes with his own.

Dr. Zellermann showed no expression whatever. He looked at the Saint woodenly, with a supreme disinterest. He might have been watching a fly he was about to swat.

"Once one understands a certain type of mind," Dr. Zellermann said almost contemptuously, "predictions of action patterns are elementary——"

"My dear Watson," the Saint supplied.

"You visited Mrs. Gerald Meldon and James Prather," Zellermann continued. "Theirs were two of the three names on my appointment pad. It follows that you also visited Foley. It was obviously you who telephoned the police—the phrasing of the message fits your psychological pattern exactly. Foley was dead when you left. The police are looking for a murderer. I knew that my office had been entered, of course, because someone answered the telephone when no one should have been there. I suspected that that 'someone' was you; and the rest followed. It was only necessary to have you confirm my deductions yourself."

The Saint's smile held a wholly irrational delight.

"I see," he said softly. "You know, Ernst, my esteem for you has raised itself by its mouldy bootstraps. I bow to you. From now on, life will have a keener edge."

"Life, if any, Templar. In spite of what you read in the papers, murderers frequently do go to the chair."

"Not this one, dear old wizard." The Saint turned to Spaniel Eyes. "Shall we begin our invasion of Sing Sing?"

"Yerk, yerk," Spaniel Eyes said.

As the Saint got to his feet, Avalon stood beside him. He looked into her dark eyes deeply and ironically. Her gaze didn't waver.

"I didn't," she whispered. "I didn't."

Simon kissed her lightly.

"Be a good girl. Don't forget to eat your vitamins."

"But you're not going like a lamb," she cried. "Aren't you even going to try to do something?"

That gay and careless smile flashed across his face. "My dear old Aunt Harriet always said that as long as there's life there's life. Thanks for the drinks, Doctor."

He was gone, walking straight as a magician's wand between Scar-chin and Spaniel Eyes. Their passage between the tables was leisurely and attracted no notice, aside from a bold and admiring glance now and then from women lunchers. They might have been three executives headed back to their marts, or three friends popping off to green and manicured pastures to chase a pellet of gutta-percha from one hole to another. Certainly no one would have suspected that the Saint was a prisoner—in fact, any speculations would have tended to reverse their rôles.

But under his calm exterior, thought processes moved at incredible speed, toying with this idea, discarding that. He didn't put it beyond himself to stage a spectacular escape as soon as they were outside; but on the other hand it would be no help to him to become a fugitive. He even wondered whether Dr. Zellermann's system of psychological projection had anticipated an attempt to escape and was even now listening with one ear for the rattle of shots which would mean that the shadow of the Saint's interference had perhaps been lifted permanently.

Simon saw too many arguments against obliging him. His best bet at the moment seemed to be discretion, watchful waiting, and the hope that the cell they gave him to try on for size would have southern exposure.

Spaniel Eyes hailed a cab. Scar-chin climbed in first, followed by the Saint, and Spaniel Eyes gave short inaudible directions to the driver.

"Well," the Saint said after a few moments of riding, "how about a swift game of gin rummy?"

"Shaddup," Spaniel Eyes said, and looked at his watch.

"By the way," Simon asked, "what are visiting hours in the local calaboza?"

"Shaddup," Spaniel Eyes said.

They rode some more. They wound through Central Park, entering at Columbus Circle, curving and twisting along the west side of that great haven for nurses, sailors, nurses and sailors, up around the bottleneck end of the lake, south past the zoo.

The Saint looked significantly at the flat backs of the animal cages. "What time," he asked Spaniel Eyes, "do you have to be back in?"

"Shaddup."

"This," the Saint said conversationally to Scar-chin, "has been most illuminating. I suppose I shouldn't ever have taken this drive otherwise. Very restful. The lake full of row-boats, the row-boats full of afternoon romance, the—oh, the *je ne sais quoi*, like kids with ice-creamed noses."

Scar-chin yawned.

Simon lighted another cigarette and brooded over the routine. He considered his chances of getting a lawyer with a writ of habeas corpus before things went too far. Or was it the scheme of Scar-chin and Spaniel Eyes to spirit him away to some obscure precinct station and hold him incommunicado? Such things had been done before. And at that stage of the game the Saint knew he could not afford to disappear even for twenty-four hours.

Spaniel Eyes looked at his watch as they neared the exit at Fifty-ninth Street and Fifth Avenue.

"Okay," he called to the cab driver.

The driver nodded and drove to—of all places—the Algonquin. Scar-chin came back to life.

"Awright," he said. "Go on up to your room."

"And then what?"

"You'll see."

Simon nodded pleasantly, and went up to his room. The telephone was ringing.

"Hamilton," said the voice at the other end. "I wish you'd be more careful. Do you think I haven't anything else to do with my men except send them to pull you out of jams?"

4

For a considerable time after the Saint had left, there was a nominal silence in the dining-room of 21. Nominal, because of course there was never any actual silence in that much-publicised pub except when it was closed for the night. The chatter of crocks, cutlery, concubines and creeps went on without interruption or change of tempo, a formless obbligato like the fiddling of insects in a tropic night which could only be heard by forced attention. It washed up against the table where Zellermann and Avalon sat, and still left them isolated in a pool of stillness.

Of Avalon one could only have said that she was thinking. Her face was intent and abstracted but without mood. If it suggested any tension, it was only by its unnatural repose.

Dr. Zellermann avoided that suggestion by just enough play with cocktail glass and cigarette, with idle glances around the room, to convey a disinterested expectation that this hiatus was purely transitory, and that he was merely respecting it with polite acceptance.

He turned to Avalon at last with a sympathetic smile.

"I'm so sorry," he said in his best tableside manner.

She shrugged.

"Sorry? For what?"

"It is not my desire, Miss Dexter, to cause you anguish or heartache."

"I've been watching out for myself for some time, Doctor."

"That, my dear, is your chief attraction. One would expect a girl who is as beautiful as you to be dependent. You have a magnificent—er—contempt for the conventional behaviour of beautiful women. If I may say so."

"You have, Doctor. Which all leads up to an exit line. Good-bye."

He raised a soft white hand.

"Don't go. You haven't had your lunch."

"I'm not hungry."

"Then please listen. I have information that may be to your advantage to know."

She settled back, but did not relax. She had the appearance of a motionless cat, not tense, yet ready to leap. Her dark eyes were alert, wide and bright.

"About Mr. Templar," the psychiatrist began. "Although I am glad to confess a personal interest in your welfare, what I am about to say is of an academic nature."

Avalon smiled with one side of her mouth.

"Anyone will grant that he is a romantic figure, Miss Dexter. He must have a tremendous attraction for women, especially young and beautiful girls who are trying to carve out a career. He represents all they strive for—poise, charm, fame and respect from many psychological types. But he is not a stable person, Miss Dexter."

Avalon smiled with both sides of her mouth. It was a tender smile, with secret undertones.

"His path through life," said Zellermann—"and I don't mean to sound like a text-book—is inevitably beset with adventure, crime, and personal danger. I happen to know that many who have allied themselves with him have died. Somehow, he has come through all his adventures. But the day will come, my dear Miss Dexter, when Lady Luck will frown on her favourite protégé."

Avalon rose abruptly.

"And so on and so on," she said. "Let's skip the soul analysis. You heard him fling me to the wolves. I informed on him, he said. I told you about what he's been doing. I don't think I'm in danger of being hurt—or even being near him, for that matter. So long."

She walked out of the hotel, straight and tall and lovely. When she was on the sidewalk, three cab drivers rushed up to claim her for a fare. She chose one.

"The Tombs," she said; and the man blinked.

"Caught up with th' boy friend, hey? 'Stoo bad, lady."

"My grandmother," Avalon said icily, "is in jail for matricide. I'm taking her a hacksaw. Will you hurry?"

All the way to the gloomy pile of stone, the cab driver shook his head. When Avalon paid him off, he looked at her with troubled eyes.

" 'Scuse me, lady, but why would the old dame steal a mattress? It don't make sense."

"She got tired of sleeping on the ground," Avalon told him. "Some people just can't take it."

She went inside and was directed to the desk sergeant. He was a large man, and the lines in his face had not been acquired by thinking up ways to help his fellow-man. He was busy at the moment she arrived before him studying some printed matter on his desk. He didn't look up.

"Excuse me," Avalon said.

The sergeant paid no attention. He continued his study of the papers before him. He held a pencil in one huge fist, and made a check mark now and then.

"I beg your pardon," Avalon said.

Still there was no evidence that the sergeant had heard her. He continued to peruse his mysterious papers. Avalon, like those who also serve, stood and waited. Presently the sergeant made a check mark after the name Sir Walter in the fourth at Pimlico and looked up.

His eyes were without expression. They roved over the convolutions of beauty as if they had been inspecting a prize farm animal. They penetrated, yes, and Avalon could feel her clothes falling off her; but there was no lust, no desire, in the sergeant's eyes—only boredom.

"Yep?" he said.

"I want to see a prisoner you have here," she said. "His name is Templar." She spelled it.

The sergeant's eyes said "Dames!" as he reached for a heavily bound ledger. He scanned it.

"When did he get here?"

"An hour ago, or less."

"Nobody's been here in the last hour."

"Where would he be, then?"

"What's the rap?"

"Oh, he hasn't even been tried. No charge has been made."

The sergeant's eyes groaned, rolled skyward.

"Lady, he'll be booked at Centre Street headquarters. He won't come here till he's been convicted."

"Oh, I didn't know. Where is it?"

He told her. She flagged a cab, and went there.

As she mounted the wide flight of stairs, she was joined by Kay Natello and Ferdinand Pairfield.

Ferdinand was resplendent in purple scarf, grey plaid jacket, dove-grey trousers, grey suède shoes and lemon-coloured socks. His hands were white butterflies emerging from cocoons.

"Darling!" he cried, like bells from *Lakmé*.

Kay Natello might as well have been dressed in a fire hose, for all the blue cotton dress did for her gaunt frame. She said nothing, and Avalon was grateful for being spared that.

"Myrmidons," Avalon murmured. "What's the rap?"

Ferdinand put butterflies on her arm and she shivered.

"Quaint girl," he purred. "We were down to see a lawyer on Wall Street, and we were just passing in a cab—with the most brutal driver, my dear, simply delicious—and Kay said 'There's Avalon!' And since we'd been looking all over for you——" His shrug was as graceful as feathers on a little wind.

"Looking for me?"

"Yes, come on," Kay Natello said, in the voice which was so like an overstrained buzz-saw.

"The most marvellous thing, darling," Ferdinand

burbled. "Magnamount's going to do a picture around Cookie's Canteen. We'll all be in it. And you're to have a good rôle. So come along. Cookie wants to be sure you'll play before she signs up with Mr. Pfeffer."

"Mr. Pfeffer being——?"

"The producer, dear girl. He's very quaint."

Avalon stood in indecision for a moment. She seemed to find nothing to say. But at last she said: "Okay. You two run along. I'll join you shortly. At Cookie's?"

"But you can't possibly," Ferdinand objected. "And surely you haven't anything to do in this dismal place. You couldn't be interested in any of the sordid characters who find their way in here. What are you doing here anyway?"

"I lost a gold compact and a pair of ear-rings out of my purse in a taxi," she said. "I thought this would be the place to report it. Not that I expect it'll do much good."

"It probably won't," Ferdinand said. "But I'll help you talk to these dreadful barbarians, and then we can all ride back up town together."

CHAPTER FOUR

How Simon Templar dressed up, and duly went to a Party

THE two young men who rang James Prather's doorbell might have been well-dressed haberdasher's assistants, shoe salesmen, or stockbrokers. They told the goggle-eyed Mr. Prather that they were attached to the Treasury Department and had credentials to prove it. One of them, a calm blond boyish young man, said his name was Harrison. He introduced the other, who was red-headed and freckled, as Smith.

Prather's pale hands fluttered in the direction of the divan.

"Sit down, will you? What's the matter? Income-tax trouble?"

Smith placed his blue felt hat on his well-pressed knee and said nothing. He seemed intensely interested in the hat. Harrison pushed his own hat back on his tow hair and seemed to develop a curiosity about the ceiling. Nobody said anything. Prather remained standing, not quite twisting his hands together; and his lobster-like eyes moved from Harrison to Smith and back.

Harrison broke the silence lazily: "You know a man named Sam Jeffries, I believe?"

Prather frowned.

"Jeffries? Jeffries? No, I think not."

"He said he was here to see you. He was quite definite about the location."

Prather frowned again.

"Oh . . . Yes. Yes, I think I remember who you mean. Yes. He was here, all right. What about him?"

Smith raised his freckled face.

"How's Shanghai these days?"

Prather blinked.

Harrison said: "Specifically, 903 Bubbling Well Road."

Prather blinked again. The effect was rather like raising and lowering a curtain rapidly over thickly curved lenses.

"I don't know what you're talking about, of course."

"Ah?" Smith said.

"Oh?" Harrison said.

"And I don't understand why the Treasury Department should be interested in me."

Harrison leaned back and looked at the far corner of the room. "I believe Sam Jeffries brought you a package—or packages?"

"Yes. He picked up a piece of carving for me in Shanghai—an old Chinese monk carrying a basket of fish. Very pretty."

"Where is it?" Smith asked.

"I—uh—I gave it to a—well, you know how it is—a girl."

"U'mm," Smith said.

"H'mm," Harrison said. "Where did you meet this Jeffries?"

"Oh—uh—you know—around—I don't remember."

Smith pushed a hand through his red hair and looked directly at Prather.

"According to the information that we have," he said, like a class valedictorian reciting, "you met Sam Jeffries for the first time in a place known as Cookie's Canteen on August 18th last year. At that time you entered into some kind of an agreement with him, which required a handshake to seal it, and he went on his way. On November 30th, Sam Jeffries met you here in this apartment and brought with him his friend, Joe Hyman. Why? What agreement did you enter into with the two of them?"

"If you two guys would give me some idea of what you're trying to find out," Prather said, "I might be able to help you. So far you haven't made any sense at all."

Harrison moved his eyes, giving the impression of a Government Man on an important job.

"Suppose you answer a few questions for a change,

Mr. Prather. We could take you down-town with us and make quite a business of this, you know."

"What goes? All you've done so far is make innuendoes. You haven't accused me of anything specific, and —well—hell! I don't like it!"

Smith turned his freckled face directly on Prather.

"What is 903 Bubbling Well Road to you? What did you say to Sam Jeffries? Who's the guy above you? How do you think you're going to get out of all this? There, my friend, are some specific questions."

James Prather's cock-lobster eyes regarded Mr. Smith with a sort of frantic intensity.

"But—but—but——"

Harrison said: "I see. Maybe you'd better come along with us, Mr. Prather."

Prather, it was quite obvious, searched his conscience, his capabilities, and appraised his ingenuity. He looked at Harrison. He looked at Smith, and his thoughts retreated into the inside of his own mind. From somewhere he gathered a certain nervous courage, and he set his mouth in a quivering line.

"I don't know what you're after, but I do know one thing. I can stand on my constitutional rights. Unless you have any formal charges to bring against me, I don't have to say anything to you. Good day, gentlemen."

"Well," Harrison said.

"Ho-hum," Smith said.

The two young men got lazily to their feet and eyed the jittering Prather without expression for a long time. Then they went away. Prather was also on his way as soon as he could get into a jacket and grab a hat. He flagged a taxi in front of the apartment house, and directed the driver to Dr. Zellermann's Park Avenue offices.

Zellermann was not happy to see him. His long face would have made ice-cubes seem like fire-crackers. He chose his words carefully, as if he were picking each one out of a hat.

"And so you led them directly to me. Mr. Prather, I consider this a very ill-advised move on your part."

"I didn't lead them to you. I wasn't followed."

"May I ask just how you know that? In your present condition you wouldn't see an elephant following you." Dr. Zellermann picked up his 'phone, and dialled a number. "Bring two of your boys with you immediately."

"What—what are you going to do?" Prather asked. He repeated the question three times.

Dr. Zellermann made a triangle with the thumb and forefingers of his two white hands, and rested his chin upon the apex. He looked at James Prather as if he were a subject being discussed by a class in zoology.

"One of the principal aims of this particular organisation, as you know, is to take care of our own. You, inadvertently, have placed us in a position where you are in danger—physically, morally, and legally. We believe that it is to the interests of the organisation to protect you. That was the purpose of my call."

"You mean then you're not——"

"Going to——"

"Well—uh——"

"Liquidate you? My dear Mr. Prather, please! As I said before, our prime motivation in these present circumstances is to take care of our own. While we are waiting, I want you to tell me exactly what you told the Government men."

James Prather's mind was a roil of emotions. Uppermost, of course, was the instinct of self-preservation. He not only had no desire to die, but his every thought was directed strictly toward keeping himself alive. He cast into his mind for motives, inferences, and implications in Dr. Zellermann's attitude which might be at odds with that inherent drive which is born into every man.

"I didn't tell them anything. They seemed to know more than you could possibly expect them to. When their questions reached a certain point, I did what I had to, and that was to clam up."

"What exactly did they seem to know about?"

"They mentioned Jeffries and Hyman. They knew that they'd visited me and brought me something from Shanghai. And they asked me if I knew 903 Bubbling Well Road."

"Which of course you denied."

"Naturally. But how would they know about Jeffries and Hyman?"

Zellermann spread his hands.

"Who can tell? Seamen with money get drunk, sometimes they get into trouble. There are all kinds of situations in which they might talk. Luckily, however, they have nothing to talk about—except yourself. And you would never be indiscreet."

Prather swallowed.

"Of course not. I know I'm worried. But if you don't let me down——"

Dr. Zellermann nodded.

"I knew we could depend upon you, Mr. Prather."

And then silence fell. Dr. Zellermann seemed to have said all that he wished to say, and James Prather was afraid to say anything more They sat quietly, not meeting each other's eye. They sat like this for an undeterminable time, and their tableau was disturbed by Dr. Zellermann's blonde secretary, with the sleekedback hair, who stuck her head into the office and said:

"Mr. Carpenter to see you with two friends."

"Show them in."

The trio who entered the office were large hard-eyed men, pushing middle-age. They had one characteristic in common: they were ready to take orders and carry them out.

"Mr. Carpenter, Mr. Prather."

The two men shook hands. Prather was nervous, Carpenter matter of fact.

"Mr. Prather," Dr. Zellermann continued, "has unfortunately attracted some undesirable attention. It's up to us to see that he comes to no harm in the hands of the authorities. Mr. Carpenter, you know what to do."

Prather stood up.

"Dr. Zellermann, I can't thank you enough. I——"

Dr. Zellermann waved away his protestations of good will.

"Nonsense. One looks out for one's own."

James Prather twiddled his thumbs nervously as the long black car wound through traffic for an hour or more and left behind the city limits of New York. At long intervals farmhouses appeared on each side, and it may be presumed that birds sang in the trees nearby. Prather had no ear for our feathered friends and no eyes for rustic architecture. He sat rigidly in the back seat between the two nameless companions of Mr. Carpenter, while that gentleman drove expertly and swiftly to their unrevealed destination. The others initiated no trivial conversation, and Mr. Prather was in no mood to start any himself.

When they had travelled another hour, Carpenter swung down a narrow side road, whose pavement gave way presently to a sandy surface. Another turning brought them into a lane which was distinguished by car tracks and overhanging maples. After a half-mile's travel along this road, Carpenter stopped the car. He got out.

"This way," he said.

Prather, not without inner misgivings, followed the big man through a barbed-wire fence, across a pasture, and deep into a green orchard of apple trees.

"Where are you taking me?" Prather asked in a small voice.

Carpenter turned to face him.

"No place," he said. "You're here."

He took an automatic from under his left arm and pointed it at Prather's chest. The first shot would have been enough; but Carpenter, a conscientious man, gave him a second bullet to make certain.

2

The man who went down the back stairs of the Algonquin Hotel and slipped quickly and inconspicuously through the lobby from the service door could never have been mistaken for the debonair and immaculate Mr. Templar who had lately become accepted as one of the brighter landmarks of that possessive caravanserai. He wore heavy black shoes that were cracked and stained and down at heel, heavy black wool socks drooping untidily over his ankles, dark blue trousers with baggy knees and a shiny seat, a soiled white shirt with a dark tie knotted and twisted like an old rope, a dark blue reefer jacket that was wrinkled across the shoulders, patched in one elbow and threadbare at the cuffs, and a vaguely nautical peaked cap without insignia that looked as if it was used to combining the functions of head-gear and brass polisher. His shoulders sagged and his chest slouched, so that he didn't seem very tall. His complexion was ruddy and weather-beaten. What could be seen of his hair was a drab grey that matched his bushy eyebrows and straggly moustache and the close-cropped fringe of beard around his chin.

He was out of the hotel so quickly that nobody really noticed him, but he was not bothered about being seen. If any leg men of the Ungodly were watching for him in the lobby, he was quite sure that they would patiently continue to sit and watch. The man who had become Tom Simons right down to his grimy finger-nails was prepared to submit his creation to any ocular inspection —including that of the door-keeper at Cookie's Canteen.

The door-keeper, who was a woman with dyed red hair and a face like a dyspeptic camel, examined his identification papers and gave him a stock smile which displayed many large teeth tastefully mounted in gold.

"Glad to have you with us, Mr. Simons," she said. "Go right in and make yourself at home."

The Saint went in.

He found himself in a big barren room which had probably once been a restaurant, for one side of it was still broken up into upholstered booths. The rest of the furnishings were less ornamental, consisting of plain bare wooden tables and chairs, all of them scarred from much service. On the side opposite the booths there was a low dais with little more than enough room for the grand piano that stood on it. The walls were plastered with posters of female nubility and cartoons from *Esquire*. Near the entrance there was a rack of tattered popular magazines. At the back of the room there was a service bar from behind which two very wavy-haired young men in their shirt-sleeves were dispensing sand-

wiches and bottles of non-alcoholic throat irrigation. A
juke box blared inexorably through the hit parade.

The room was crowded with men of all ages, some
in ordinary civilian clothes, some in costumes that tried
nebulously to look like a sort of seafaring uniform. Some
of the parties at the tables were engrossed in games of
cards or checkers. Other men danced with the hostesses
in a clear space in front of the piano, clumsily or stiffly
or flashily according to type. The hostesses were mostly
young and pert and passably good-looking. They wore
aprons with star-dotted borders and *Cookie's Canteen*
embroidered across them. A few other smooth-skinned
young men in identical aprons moved among the tables
picking up empty bottles and dirty plates.

Aside from the rather noticeably sleek fragility of the
male helpers, the place was fairly typical of the numer-
ous oases that had mushroomed across the country
during the war to offer chaste and sheltered recreation
to men of the services, in line with the current con-
cept of tea and parlour games as the great spiritual
need of a warrior between battles. But whereas practically all the prototypical estaminets were sponsored
and protected by public organisations, Cookie's Canteen
was a strictly free-lance and unofficial and unendorsed
post-war benevolence. And in all of that there were
questions to which the Saint wanted many answers. . . .

He edged his way through the tables to the service
bar and asked for a coke. With the bottle in his hand,
he turned back toward the room, scanning the crowd
through the thick fog of smoke that hung under the
low ceiling and wondering what his move should be.

A girl in an apron stopped in front of him.

"Hello," she said. "You got everything you want?"

"Yus, thank yer, miss."

"Gee, you must be English."

"That's right, miss." The Saint's voice was hoarse and innocent. "Strite from Aldgate. 'Ow did yer guess?"

"Oh, I'm getting so I can spot all the accents."

"Well now!" said the Saint admiringly.

"This your first time here?"

"Yus, miss."

"When did you get to New York?"

"Just got in larst night."

"Well, you didn't take long to find us. Do you have any friends here?"

"No, miss. . . ."

The Saint was just saying it when a face caught his eye through the blue haze. The man was alone now in a booth which a couple of other seamen had just left, and as he shifted his seat and looked vacantly around the room the Saint saw him clearly and recognised him.

He said suddenly: "Gorblimy, yes I do! I know that chap dahn there. Excuse me, miss——"

He jostled away through the mob and squeezed unceremoniously into the booth, plonking his bottle down on the stained table top in front of him.

"Ullo, mite," he said cheerfully. "I know I've seen you before. Your nime's Patrick 'Ogan, ain't it?"

"Shure, Hogan's the name," said the other genially, giving him a square view of the unmistakable pug-nosed physiognomy which Simon had last seen impaled on the spotlight of Cookie's Cellar. "An' what's yours?"

"Tom Simons."

"I don't remember, but think nothing of it. Where was it we met?"

"Murmansk, I think——durin' the war?"

"It's just as likely. Two weeks I've spent there on two trips, an' divil a night sober."

It appeared that Hogan found this a happy and satisfactory condition, for he had obviously taken some steps already toward inoculating himself against the evils of sobriety. His voice was a little slurred, and his breath was warmed with spicier fluids than passed over the counter of Cookie's Canteen.

"This 'ere's a bit off orl right, ain't it?" Simon said, indicating the general surroundings with a wave of his bottle.

"There's nothing better in New York, Tom. An' that Cookie—she's a queen, for all she sings songs that'd make your own father blush."

"She is, is she?"

"Shure she is, an' I'll fight any man that says she isn't. Haven't ye heard her before?"

"Naow. Will she be 'ere ter-night?"

"Indeed she will. Any minute now. That's what I come in for. If it wasn't for her, I'd rather have a drink that'll stay with me an' a girl I can have to meself to roll in the hay. But Cookie can take care of that too, if she's a friend of yours."

He winked broadly, a happy pagan with a girl and a hang-over in every port.

"Coo," said the Saint, properly impressed. "And are yer a friend off 'ers?"

"You bet I am. Why, last Saturday she takes me an' a friend o' mine out to that fine club she has, an' gives us all the drinks we can hold; an' there we are livin' like lords until daybreak, an' she says any time we want to go back we can do the same. An' if you're a friend o' mine, Tom, why, she'll do the same for you."

"Lumme," said the Saint hungrily. "Jer fink she would?"

"Indeed she will. Though I'm surprised at an old man like you havin' these ideas."

"I ain't so old," said the Saint aggrievedly. "And if it comes ter 'aving fun wif a jine——"

A figure loomed over the table and mopped officiously over it with a checkered rag. The hand on the rag was pale and long-fingered, and Simon noticed that the finger-nails were painted with a violet-tinted lacquer.

Hardly daring to believe that anything so good could be true, the Saint let his eyes travel up to the classical features and pleated golden hair of the owner of that exotic manicure.

It was true. It was Ferdinand Pairfield.

Mr. Pairfield looked at the Saint, speculatively, but without a trace of recognition; discarded him, and smirked at the more youthful and rugged-looking Hogan.

"Any complaints, boys?" he asked whimsically.

"Yes," Hogan said flatly. "I don't like the help around here."

Mr. Pairfield pouted.

"Well, you don't have to be *rude*," he said huffily, and went away.

"The only thing wrong with this place," Hogan observed sourly, "is all those pretty boys. I dunno why they'd be lettin' them in, but they're always here."

Then the truculent expression vanished from his face as suddenly as it had come there, and he let out a shrill joyful war-cry.

"Here she is, Tom," he whooped. "Here's Cookie!"

The lights dimmed as he was speaking, giving focus

to the single spotlight that picked up the bulbous figure of Cookie as she advanced to the front of the dais.

Her face was wide open in the big hearty jolly beam that she wore to work. Throwing inaudible answers back to the barrage of cheers and whistling that greeted her, she manœuvred her hips around the piano and settled them on the piano stool. Her ploughman's hands pounded over the keyboard; and the Saint leaned back and prepared himself for another parade of her merchandise.

"Good evening, everybody," she blared when she could be heard. "Here we are again, with a load of those songs your mothers never taught you. To-night we'll try and top them all—as usual. Hold on to your pants, boys, and let's go!"

She went.

It was a performance much like the one that Simon had heard the night before; only much more so. She took sex into the sewer and brought it out again, dripping. She introduced verses and adlibs of the kind that are normally featured only at stag smokers of the rowdiest kind. But through it all she glowed with that great gargoyle joviality that made her everybody's broad-minded big sister; and to the audience she had, much as the U.S.O. would have disapproved and the Y.M.C.A. would have turned pale with horror, it was colossal. They hooted and roared and clapped and beat upon the tables, demanding more and more until her coarse homely face was glistening with the energy she was pouring out. And in key with his adopted character, and to make sure of retaining the esteem of Patrick Hogan, the Saint's enthusiasm was as vociferous as any.

It went on for a full three-quarters of an hour before Cookie gave up, and then Simon suspected that her principal reason was plain exhaustion. He realised that she was a leech for applause: she soaked it up like a sponge, it fed and warmed her, and she gave it back like a kind of transformed incandescence. But even her extravagant stamina had its limit.

"That's all for now," she gasped. "You've worn me down to a shadow." There was a howl of laughter. "Come back to-morrow night, and I'll try to do better."

She stepped down off the platform to be hand-shaken and slapped on the back by a surge of admirers as the lights went up again.

Patrick Hogan climbed to his feet, pushing the table out and almost upsetting it in his eagerness. He cupped his hands to his mouth and split the general hubbub with a stentorian shout.

"Hey, Cookie."

His coat was rucked up to his hips from the way he had been sitting, and as lurched there his right hip pocket was only a few inches from Simon's face. Quite calmly and almost mechanically the Saint's eyes traced the outlines of the object that bulged in the pocket under the rough cloth—even before he moved to catch a blue-black gleam of metal down in the slight gape of the opening.

Then he lighted a cigarette with extreme thoughtfulness, digesting the new and incontrovertible fact that Patrick Hogan, that simple spontaneous child of nature, was painting the town with a roscoe in his pants.

3

Cookie sat down with them, and Hogan said: "This is me friend Tom Simons, a foine sailor an' an old goat with the gals. We were drunk together in Murmansk —or I was drunk anyway."

"How do you do, Tom," Cookie said.

"Mustn't grumble," said the Saint. " 'O's yerself?"

"Tired. And I've still got two shows to do at my own place."

"I certainly did enjoy 'earing yer sing, ma'm."

"This your first visit?"

"Yus, ma'm."

"Call me Cookie. Everyone does."

"Yus, ma'm."

"I bet it won't be his last," Hogan said. "Eh, Tom?"

"Not arf it won't," said the Saint. "If you'll 'ave me. But I dunno as I'll 'ave a lot more charnces on this trip."

Cookie took out a pack of cigarettes, offered them, and lit one for herself. She looked at the Saint again.

"Aren't you staying long?" she added conversationally.

"Naow. Back on board by supper-time on Tuesday, them's the orders—an' we only drops the 'ook yesterdye. Be a s'ilor an' see the world—I don't think."

"That's too bad."

"Aow, it's orl in the dye's work, ma'm. But I ses ter meself, I'm goin' ter see New York while I got the charnce, by crikey."

"Where are you heading for next?"

"Through the canal an' strite to Shanghai. Then back from there to 'Frisco. Then——"

"Say, Cookie," interrupted Hogan brazenly, "how's about a drop of real liquor for a couple o' good friends who've dried their throats to a cinder with cheerin' for ye?"

She took a deep man-sized drag at her cigarette, flicked ash from it on to the table, and glanced at the

Saint again with expressionless and impersonal calculation.

"I might find you a drop," she said.

She stood up and started away; and Patrick Hogan nudged the Saint with one of his broad disarming winks as they followed her.

"What did I tell ye, Tom?"

"Cor," said the Saint appreciatively, "you ain't arf a one."

They went through a door at the side of the service bar, which took them into a kitchen that might once have been bustling and redolent with the concoction of rare dishes for the delectation of gourmets. Now it looked bare and drab and forlorn. There was no one there. A centre table was piled with loaves of bread and stacks of sliced ham and cheese, and littered with crumbs and scraps. Cases of coke and pop were pyramided in one corner. The only thing on the stove was an enormous steaming coffee pot; and a mass of dirty cups and plates raised sections of their anatomy, like vestiges of a sunken armada, out of the lake of greasy water in the sink.

Cookie led the way into another room that opened off the kitchen. It was so tiny that it must once have seen duty as a store room. Now it barely had space for a couple of plain chairs, a waste-basket, a battered filing cabinet, and a scarred desk scattered with bills and papers. Kay Natello sat at the desk, in front of an antique typewriter, pecking out an address on an envelope with two clawlike fingers.

"Hullo, Kay," Hogan said familiarly. "An' how's me swateheart to-night?"

"We're just going to have a quick one," Cookie said. "Be a darling and find us some glasses, Kay, will you?"

Kay Natello got up and went out into the kitchen, and Cookie opened a drawer of the desk and pulled out a half-empty bottle of Scotch. Natello came back with four wet glasses and put them on the desk.

"This is Tom Simons—Kay Natello," Cookie said. "Tom's only just got in, and he's sailing again on Tuesday."

"Too bad," said Natello.

"We all 'ave ter work, Miss," Simon said modestly. "At least we got plenty o' grub an' a nice clean bed ter sleep in, as long as it don't sink under us."

Cookie finished pouring four powerful slugs, and picked up one of them.

"Well, boys," she said. "Down the hatch."

The drinks duly went down the hatch.

"You were sailing soon, too, weren't you, Pat?" asked Natello.

"Next week. Off to South Africa, India, Singapore, and back the same way."

"We'll miss you," said Cookie. "What about you, Tom—are you going to England?"

"Shanghai," said the Saint, wiping his droopy moustache. "Through the canal an' back to 'Frisco."

Cookie poured herself another drink, and downed it at one gulp like a dose of medicine. Perhaps that was what it was for her.

"I've got to leave you," she announced. "Got my next show to do."

She helped herself to another small jolt, as an afterthought, just in case she had made a mistake and cheated herself on the last one. The effect on her was not even noticeable. Her small piggy eyes summarised the Saint with the quick covert shrewdness of an adept Fifty-second Street head waiter taking the measure of a new

customer. She said with perfectly timed spontaneity:
"Look, why don't you boys come over to the Cellar
when you get through here? On the house."

Hogan thumped her heartily on the back without
even jarring her.

"Darlin', what did ye think we were waitin' for?
Sure, we'll be there shoutin' for ye. Won't we, Tom?"

"Crikey," said the Saint, with a wistful break in his
voice. "You ain't arf giving us a time, ma'm. I mean,
Cookie."

"That's fine," Cookie said. "Then I'll be expecting
you. Kay, you take care of them and bring them along.
See you all later."

She gathered her foundation around her, gave a last
hesitant glance at the Scotch bottle and made a reso-
lute exit like a hippopotamus taking off to answer the
call of Spring.

Kay Natello took care of them.

Simon didn't keep very close track of the caretaking,
but the general trend of it was quite simple. After the
Scotch was finished and they left the canteen, it in-
volved stopping at a great many bars on the way and
having a drink or two in each of them. Hogan acquired
more blarney and boisterousness as it went on: he said
that Kay was his girl, and an Irishman's girl was his
castle, or something that sounded like that. He beam-
ingly offered to pulverise various persons whom he
suspected of dissenting from his opinions about Oliver
Cromwell, Michael Collins, De Valera, and Kay Natello.
Simon Templar did his best to keep in time with the
mood, and surreptitiously dribbled as many drinks as
he could into the nearest cuspidor. Through it all, Kay
Natello only became more stringy and more removed.
She responded to Pat Hogan's elephantine flirtations

when she remembered to; in between, she was more like a Y.W.C.A. chaperon trying to keep up with the girls. Simon was quite relieved that she didn't at any point offer to break into significant *vers libre*. . . . But it still seemed to take a long time to reach Cookie's Cellar.

Once they were there, however, it was a repetition of the night before from another viewpoint. This time, the Saint was one of the reluctant heroes under the spotlight. Cookie sang the same kind of songs, giving and receiving the same enthusiasm.

After one of the more turbid numbers, Kay Natello nudged the Saint and said proudly: "I wrote that for her."

"Cor!" said the Saint respectfully.

That was only a mild expression of what he thought. The idea of a poetess of Kay Natello's school composing those kinds of lyrics in her lighter moments had an austere magnificence which he hoped to dwell on some quiet evening when he had nothing else at all to do.

It was like the night before again, with a difference, because Avalon Dexter was there.

She wasn't there to work. She was just another customer, wearing a simple afternoon dress, sitting at a table at the back of the room; but he saw her long tawny hair dance as she talked and looked around. It gave him a queer sensation to watch her like that and have her glance pass over him in complete unawareness. It was like being invisible.

And it also gave him a sort of guilty feeling, as though he was hiding and spying on her. Which at that moment he was.

The man with her was slightly rotund and slightly

bald. He wore horn-rimmed glasses and he had a round and pleasant pink face that looked very clean and freshly barbered. He was not, you could tell very quickly, another Dr. Zellermann in his manual recreations. He behaved like a nice wholesome middle-aged man who was enjoying the company he was in. Any impartial observer would have conceded that he was entitled to that, and quite undeserving the unreasonable malignance with which Simon regarded him. Simon knew it was unreasonable, but that didn't blunt the stab of resentment that went through him when he saw her chattering so gaily with this complacent jerk. He was surprised at his own symptoms, and not too pleased about them either.

Cookie finished at last, with Hogan and the Saint competing in the uproariousness of their appreciation. The melancholy waiter brought some more drinks, bowed down into profounder misery by the knowledge that this was one table which he dared not discourage, and that at the same time it was one table where the tip would certainly be no compensation. Cookie ploughed through the room, stopping to give jovial greeting to various tables, and surged on to the bar, where there were other members of her following to be saluted, and the bar-tender had been trained to have three ounces of Scotch waiting for her with a cube of ice in it.

It was twenty minutes before she breasted back to her own table, and then she had Dr. Ernst Zellermann in tow.

Cookie introduced him, and mopped her face and reached for the first drink that arrived.

"Tom's sailing on Tuesday," she said. "Shanghai."

The Saint had already begun to let it look as if his

liquor consumption was catching up with him. He lurched in his chair, spilt some of his drink, and gave a wink that was getting heavy and bleary.

"Gonna find aht if it's true abaht China," he said.

"I may be able to tell you a few places to go," Zellermann said smoothly. "I spent quite a time there once —in the good days before the war."

He looked very noble and full of unfathomable memories; and Simon Templar, dimly returning his gaze, felt coldly and accurately like a specimen on a dissecting table.

Zellermann picked up his glass and turned to Cookie with the utmost charm.

"You know," he said, "I don't know why you don't invite more people like Mr. Hogan and Mr. Simons out to Long Island. After all, they deserve to be entertained much more than I do."

"That's an idea," Cookie said. "How about it, boys? I've got a little shack on the beach at Southampton. We close this joint on Sundays, anyhow. Why don't you come along? I'll see that you're back in town on Monday. You can swim in the ocean and get some sun on the beach, and we'll make a party of it and it won't cost you a cent. Dr. Zellermann and I will drive you out as soon as we've closed this place. We'll have a grand week-end. I'll have company for you, too. The most attractive girl you've ever seen." Simon was much too drunk to catch the glance that flashed between them —or at least he had been able to convince everyone of that. "Dexter is coming along," Cookie said.

4

The Saint mumbled something about seeing a man about a dog, and was able to get out alone. There was a telephone booth near the entrance. He called the Algonquin and asked for Avalon.

Miss Dexter was not there at the moment, as he knew; but could they take a message?

"When is she likely to get it?" he asked.

"I couldn't say, sir, but she's been calling in about every half-hour. She seems to be expecting a message. Is this Mr. Templar?"

The Saint held his breath for a moment, and took a lightning decision.

"Yes."

"I know she's asked whether you called. Can she call you back?"

The Saint said: "I'm afraid she can't reach me, but tell her I'll see her to-morrow."

Nothing could have been more true than that, even if she didn't understand it; and somehow it made him feel better with himself. It meant something to know that she had hoped he would find a way to get in touch with her—no matter why. She would not know that he had been back to the Algonquin since his "arrest," for that had been taken care of; and she must continue to believe that he was locked up somewhere down-town. But she had asked . . .

Both of them had become hooked to an unwinding chain that was going somewhere on its own. Only it happened to be the same chain for both of them. It seemed as if the hand of destiny was in that—Simon didn't want to think any more, just then, about what that destiny might be.

When he got back to the table, everything had been settled. Patrick Hogan proclaimed that when his great-grandfather sailed for America, all the luggage he had was in his coat pockets, and he could do anything that his great-grandfather could do. He was certain that, next to his great-grandfather and himself, his pal Tom Simons was just as expert at light travelling.

"I can take you in my car," Zellermann said convivially. "There's plenty of room."

Simon didn't doubt it was a car you could play badminton in.

"I'll have to stay till the bitter end," said Cookie, "and Dexter will probably want to pick up some things. I'll bring her."

It was worked out just as easily and rapidly as that. But Simon knew that aside from the hospitable co-operation, Avalon Dexter was not intended to know that Dr. Zellermann would be a member of the house party. Or he hoped he knew it.

He had some confirmation of that when they were leaving. Avalon seemed to be on her way back from the powder room when they started out. There was a rather lost and apart expression on her face that no one else might have seen. Zellermann half stopped her.

"Good evening, Avalon," he said, half formally and half engagingly.

"How are you?" Avalon said, very brightly and very cheerfully and without a pause, so that before he could have said anything else she was neatly past him and gone.

Zellermann stood looking after her without a ripple of reaction, his face as smooth as a head of marble.

Simon recalled that he had also hit Dr. Zellermann in the eye, and realised that some momentary inaccuracy had made him fail to leave any souvenir contusion on the eyelid. All he could detect, in the brighter light of the foyer, was a small area of matt surface just above the cheekbone. Dr. Zellermann's peripalpebral

ecchymosis, clearly, had received the most skilled medical and cosmetic treatment.

The encounter had made Hogan and the Saint drift
farther on toward the door, and Kay Natello had ex-
cused herself on a farewell visit to the powder room.
It was a chance that might not recur very quickly.

Simon said: "Pat, 'oo is this Dexter jine?"

"She used to work here, Tom me boy, an' a swate
singer she was too. That was her just went by. But you'll
meet her when we get to Southampton. An' if Cookie
says she's for you, ye're in luck."

"She's a corker, orl right," said the Saint. "If that's
'oo yer mean. Although she wouldn't 'ave much time
fer an ole goat like me. Clarss, that's wot she is . . ."
He staggered just a little, and put his arm around
Hogan's broad shoulders, and decided to take a chance
on Hogan's unpredictable pugnacity. "But if it comes ter
that, mite, wot djer see in an ole sack o' bones like that
there Natello?"

Hogan laughed loudly and clung to him for mutual
support.

"She's okay, Tom," he said generously. "An' she's a
friend of Cookie's, an' she's me swateheart. Is it her
fault if she's an old sack o' bones? She reminds me of
me old Aunt Eileen, an' she's been kindness itself to
me iver since we met, so I'll fight any man that says
she's not the toast 'o the town."

That was how they piled into Dr. Zellermann's car,
which was not only big enough to play badminton in
but could probably have accommodated a social set of
tennis as well.

Hogan and Natello sat in the back, and after a few
lines of noisy repartee seemed to get close together and
go to sleep. Dr. Zellermann steered them out over the

Triborough Bridge with surgical care and precision, while he chatted urbanely about the sea and world commerce and logistics and the noble part that was being played by such unsung paladins of reconversion as Tom Simons. The Saint sat beside him, making the right answers as best he could improvise them, and remembering Avalon Dexter and many various things.

Apparently, as he had worked it out, Avalon's arrival at Southampton to find Zellermann there already was meant to be a surprise for her. Apparently, then, there was an idea extant that she wouldn't have accepted the invitation if she had known Zellermann would be there. Certainly she had brushed him off coolly enough that night, with merely conventional politeness. That was what any ordinary person would think.

But Simon Templar was still alive for no more fundamental reason than that he had never thought what any ordinary person would think—or was intended to think. So that he could stand far back and see that if he were the Ungodly and he wanted to hook Simon Templar, he might easily play the cards something like that.

And why had Avalon accepted the invitation anyhow?

The Saint's lips hardened over the reminder that he always had to think like that. He had had to do it for so long that it was a habit now. And now, for the first time in an infinitude of years, he was conscious of it again.

And it wasn't any fun at all, and there was no pleasure at all in the knowledge of his own wisdom and vigilance; because this was Avalon, and this wasn't the way he wanted to think about Avalon.

Avalon with her russet locks tossing like the woods of New England in the fall, and her brown eyes that laughed so readily and looked so straight.

But Patrick Hogan with his ingenuous joviality and the gun on his hip. Patrick Hogan with his uninhibited young sailor's zest for a spree, and his cheerful acceptance of Kay Natello. Patrick Hogan, whom the Saint had hooked so deftly as a sponsor—who had been so very willing to be hooked.

And the Parkway stretching ahead, and the soothing murmurs of movement.

And Avalon with the friendliness and the passion meeting at her mouth, and the music always in her voice.

And the great hospitality of Cookie and Zellermann, and the glances that went between them.

And the headlights reaching out to suck in the road.

And Avalon . . .

The Saint slept.

He woke up presently out of a light dream mist in which sane thought and diaphanous fantasy had blended so softly and lightly that it seemed like a puzzle in clairvoyance to separate them.

Then, as you sat still and probed for them, they slipped away elusively and faded at the last finger-tip of apprehension, so that it was like searching for shadows with a lantern; and in the end there was nothing at all except time gone by and the headlights still drinking up the road—a road over which pools of thin white fog loomed intermittently and leapt and swallowed them and were gone like a dream.

The Saint lighted a cigarette and glanced at the pale precise sharply-graven profile of Dr. Zellermann on his left.

"We're nearly there," Zellermann said, as if there had been no hiatus at all.

Houses and hedges rose at the headlights, dodged adroitly, and were left behind. Southampton, Long Island, slept in peace, exposing nothing in common with its parent town of Southampton, England—not bombed, not scarred by war, and not knowing the other battle that swept through it in the sleek car that Dr. Zellermann drove.

They touched the end of Main Street, turned right and then left again presently, and then after a little while they swung into a driveway and stopped. Simon knew where they were—somewhere in the long line of ambitious beach-fronted houses which had expanded along that coast.

Cookie's summer hide-away may have been only a shanty in new shanty town, but her description of it as "a little shack" was rather modest. Dr. Zellermann let them in with a key, and found light switches with familiar assurance. They went through a panelled hall with quite a broad oak staircase, and into a living-room that was almost as big as Cookie's Cellar—which didn't make a barn of it either. But it was still a large room, with tall french windows on the ocean side and glass tables and big square-cut modern couches, all of it reflecting the kind of fast-moneyed life which Simon could easily associate with the profits of a joint like Cookie's. And probably also, reflecting, he thought in a flash of intuition the interior decorating ideas of Ferdinand Pairfield—after the apotheosis of Kay Natello he doubted whether any of the members of Cookie's clique would be allowed to withhold their talents from practical application.

Zellermann slid aside a pair of pale green mirrors

with geometrical designs frosted on them, disclosing a bar alcove with three chrome-legged stools in front and a professional array of bottles forming a relief mural behind. He stepped through the flap in the counter and said: "How about a drink?"

"Sure, an' that must have been what me throat was tryin' to tell me," said Hogan with a prodigious yawn, "when I was dreamin' about the Suez Canal on the way."

"I'll get some ice," said Natello, in the same lifeless twang, as if she was used to being useful and didn't think about it any more.

"And I'll help ye, if ye'll lead the way."

They went out. Simon sat on one of the stools, put one elbow on the bar, and pushed back his disreputable cap. Zellermann set out a row of glasses, disregarded the finely representative stock behind him, and brought up a bottle of Old MacSporran Genuine Jersey City Scotch Whisky from under the bar and began to measure out doses.

"Are you and Patrick on the same ship?" he asked pleasantly.

"Naow," said the Saint. "We met in Murmansk."

"Of course. I should have remembered. He's going to Singapore and you're headed for Shanghai."

"That's right, guv'nor."

"Have you known Patrick long?"

"Only since the larst bar we was in. In Murmansk, that was."

"Until you met at the Canteen to-night."

"That's right. An' I ses to 'im, Gorblimy, I ses, I've seen you before; an' 'e ses to me, Gorblimy, 'e ses——"

Simon went on with this.

Dr. Zellermann finished his general pouring, turned

for a liqueur glass, and unobtrusively selected himself a bottle of Benedictine from the display shelves.

"A very fine instinctive type," he said suavely. "Quite unrepressed, given to violent mental and physical expression, but essentially sequacious under the right guidance."

The Saint rubbed his eyes.

"Blimey, guv'nor," he said, "yer carn't arf tork, can yer? Strike me pink!"

He subsided into abashment when this miracle failed to occur, and devoted himself to the exotic nuances of Old MacSporran as soon as Hogan and Natello returned with sufficient ice to numb his palate into by-passing its more caustic overtones. He had a gift of being able to let time slide over him while he pretended to be linked with it, so that nobody noticed that his presence was somewhere else while he sat where he was. He was able to pass that knack on to Tom Simons, without making any change in the character he had created. But he had no important recollections of the next hour and more. He knew that Dr. Zellermann was a flawless temporary host, dispensing adequate drams of MacSporran while he sipped Benedictine; that Patrick Hogan sang "Danny Boy" and "Did Your Mother Come from Ireland?" in a very uncertain tenor; and that Kay Natello made her original drink last all the time, with her head obligingly tilted on to Hogan's shoulder and a rapt expression on her sallow face as if she had been mentally composing an elegy on the death of a gonococcus.

And then there was a rush of machinery on the drive, and an involuntary lull, and the thud of the front door, and footsteps, and the barge-like entrance of Cookie. Followed by Avalon Dexter.

Followed, after another moment, by Ferdinand Pairfield, who had apparently been swept up en route. But Simon paid scarcely any attention to him.

His eyes were on Avalon.

Her glance skimmed the room, and she saw Zellermann. She checked for the barest instant—it was so slight that it could have made no impression on anyone else. But the Saint was watching, and he saw it. And then she was still smiling, but her vivacity was skilled and watchful. Or so it seemed to him.

"Oh, company," she said, and flopped down on the sofa where Hogan and Natello were ensconced, and began chattering brightly and trivially to Hogan about night clubs and songs and bands.

Zellermann poured two drinks behind the bar, choosing the best bottles, and brought them out. He handed one to Cookie on his way, and carried the other over to Avalon.

"Since we have to be guests together," he said ingratiatingly, "couldn't we stop feuding and forgive each other?"

Avalon had to look up to him because he was on the arm of the sofa next to her.

"I'm being framed," she announced, very brightly. She dropped her voice after the general statement, but the Saint was still listening. She said: "I'll stop feuding and forgive you if you'll just get off my arm."

She went on bibbering to Hogan about musical trivia.

Simon Templar seized the opportunity to slip behind the bar, single out a bottle of Peter Dawson, and pour himself a nightcap that would last.

When he looked for Zellermann again, the doctor was standing beside Cookie with his attentive and invariable smile.

Patrick Hogan was trying to show Avalon how to sing "When Irish Eyes Are Smiling."

Zellermann was saying: " . . . to-morrow will be soon enough."

"There's plenty of time," Cookie said.

They started toward the bar.

Mr. Pairfield had already drifted over there in a rather forlorn way—perhaps because nobody was offering him any immediate appreciation, and perhaps because of an understandable reluctance to invite any more of Hogan's uninhibited hostility. He had made another distasteful survey of the Saint's well-aged uncouthness, and averted his pure pretty face to review the colour scheme of fluids and labels on the background shelves.

"I wonder," he muttered, with almost pathetic audibility, "if I'm in the mood for some Crème Violette?"

Simon didn't violently detest Mr. Pairfield, and all his instincts were against wasting gratuitous abuse on such creatures; but he was irrevocably playing a part, and he was still sure that Hogan was the star to which his wagon had to stay hitched until a better form of traction came along.

"Wot?" he said sourly. "Ain't there no Cream Pansiette 'ere?"

Mr. Pairfield was emboldened by his surroundings to tilt an offended nose.

He said superciliously: "I beg your pardon?"

"You 'eard," growled the Saint trenchantly, in the time-honoured formula of Cockney repartee. "You ain't got clorf ears."

That was when Cookie and Dr. Zellermann arrived.

Cookie said overwhelmingly: "Ferdy, don't be so sensitive. Tom's got a right to enjoy himself——"

Dr. Zellermann sidled behind the bar and leaned over toward the Saint and said with his monastic charm: "You know, in my studies of psychology nothing has ever fascinated me so much as the symbolism of the sailor. Of course you've heard all that stuff about the 'girl in every port' and 'what shall we do with the drunken sailor?' and so on. Really a fine synopsis of the natural impetuous life. But why? . . . You have a proverb which says there is no smoke without fire. Then where is the fire? The sailor—the sea. The sea, which once covered the whole earth. The sea, out of which our earliest protoplasmic ancestors first crawled to begin the primitive life which you and I are now enlarging . . ."

The Saint gaped at him with adoring incomprehension.

Cookie was absent-mindedly pouring herself another year or two of Old MacSporran, and saying to Mr. Pairfield: "Now for God's sake, Ferdy, have some Violette and stop fussing. And then you can be a good boy and see if the beds are all ready, there's a dear."

"Now take your own case, Tom," Zellermann was pursuing engagingly. "When you get to Shanghai, for instance——"

There was a sudden mild crash as Patrick Hogan spilled two glasses and an ash-tray off the table in front of him in the act of hoisting himself to his feet.

"I'm goin' to the little sailor boy's room," he proclaimed loudly.

"Second door on your right down the hall," said Kay Natello, as if she had been reciting it all her life.

"Run along, Ferdy," Cookie was saying with a certain kindness, "and see if you can't think what we ought to do about those pictures in the dining-room."

"Iver since I was born," Hogan challenged the whole world, "a little sailor boy's room has been in the sea. An' what was good enough for Nelson is good enough for me."

He hauled the drapes away from one of the french windows and began fumbling stubbornly with the door latch.

Pairfield the Unconvincible went over to help him, drew the curtains together again, and then slipped timidly out into the garden after him.

"When you get to Shanghai," Zellermann resumed blandly, "as soon as you go ashore, the first thing you'll want is a drink, and after that a girl. During your stay there you'll probably have many drinks and many girls. But you will have no furtive feeling about these girls, as you would have at home. On the contrary, you'll boast about them. Because you are a sailor, and therefore girls are your traditional privilege. Have you been to Shanghai before?"

"Naow. This'll be the fust time." Simon leered at the doctor familiarly. "But don't fergit—yer promised ter gimme some 'phone numbers."

"I won't forget," Zellermann reassured him, with all the soothing earnestness that he would have tendered to a patient with an A. A. Dun & Bradstreet. "Although most of them have probably changed since the war. However, I will put you in touch with a friend of mine who'll take good care of you. I know you'll find him, because I heard from him just the other day."

"Knows all the numbers, does 'e?"

"All of them. A very interesting fellow. He used to send me art pieces for my collection. As a matter of fact, you might be able to bring some back for me— he wrote me that he had several things that I wanted, if he could only send them."

The Saint took another drink while he weighed what chance he should take. And he knew that he had to take it. The invitation might not come again.

"Too 'ot fer the post office, eh?" he ventured encouragingly.

"Not at all. I think you'd find them very dull. But there are still so many restrictions about importing antiques——"

"Just an honest spot o' smugglin', wot?" The Saint screwed up one eye in another ponderous wink. "Well, guv'nor, Tom Simons is yer man. To 'ell wiv the customs, that's wot I always sye."

Dr. Zellermann stared at him contemplatively.

At which second the window curtains flew apart like the portals of some explosive genesis, permitting the irruptive return of Ferdinand Pairfield accompanied by a blood-curdling wail of horrific anguish which had started in the outside distance and arrived in the room with him before anyone else had been able to identify and classify it.

Mr. Pairfield was a remarkable sight, too. He was practically naked. His coat and shirt had been split down the back, so that the two halves of them hung and flapped like limp wings around his wrists. His trousers had completely disappeared, thus revealing that he wore pale jade silk drawers with his initials embroidered on them.

He ran to Cookie like a little boy running to his mother.

"Cookie!" he bawled. "That *dreadful* man! He tore my clothes, and he—he threw me into—into a lot of poison ivy!"

In that immortal moment, before anyone else could say anything, Patrick Hogan strode through the window like a victorious hooligan, beaming across every inch of his irresponsible pug-nosed face.

"Shure, an' I was just waitin' for the chance," he said

joyfully. He lurched over to the bar, still with the same broad grin, and put his left hand on the Saint's shoulder and turned him a little. "But as for you, Tom me boy, ye're no pal o' mine to have sent him afther me, bad cess to ye; an' if that's your idea of a joke, here's something that oughta tickle ye——"

Without the slightest additional warning, and while he was still grinning and stirring the Saint's shoulder with his other hand, his right fist rammed upward at the Saint's jaw. Simon Templar was caught where he sat, flat back and relaxed and utterly off his guard. There was an evanescent splash of multi-coloured flares in the centre of his head, and then a restful blackness in which sleep seemed the most natural occupation.

CHAPTER FIVE

How Ferdinand Pairfield was surprised, and Simon Templar left him

HE woke up in a very gradual and laborious way that was like dragging his mind out of a quagmire, so that although he knew in advance that he had been knocked out there was a lot of other history to struggle through before he got to thinking about that. He remembered everything that he had been through since the beginning of the story—Cookie's Cellar and Sutton Place South, the Algonquin and a cheap second-hand clothing store, Cookie's Canteen and a drive out to Southampton. He remembered people—Cookie, Natello, Pairfield, a melancholy waiter, even Wolcott Gibbs. And a girl called Avalon. And a hostess in Cookie's Canteen, and Patrick Hogan who had so much breezy fun and carried a gun on his hip—and who had socked him. And Dr. Ernst Zellermann with his clean white hair and ascetic features and persuasive voice, betraying himself with his long ponderous words and the incurable cumbersome Teutonic groping for far-fetched philosophical gener- alisations which belonged so obviously in a Germanic institute of Geopolitik. Zellermann, who was a phony refugee and a genuine master of the most painstakingly efficient technique that the same Germanic thorough- ness had ever evolved. Zellermann, who was the prime reason why the Saint had ever entered that circle at all. . . .

That was how Simon had to build it back, filling in the certainties where there had been questions before, in a dull, plodding climb out of the fog.

He didn't open his eyes at once because there was a sort of ache between his temples which made him screw up his brows in protest, or as a counter-irritant; and that made opening the eyes an independent operation to be plotted and toiled over. It came to him out of this that he had been knocked out before, seldom with a bare fist, but several times with divers blunt instruments; but the return to consciousness had never been so lag- ging and sluggish as this. He had been drugged before, and this was more like that.

After that stage, and deriving from it, there was a period of great quiet, in which he reviewed other things. He tested his sensations for the drag or the pressure of a gun anywhere on him, and remembered that he had held so strictly to his created character that he had set out unarmed. Still without moving, he let his skin give him tactile confirmation of the clothes in which he had left the Algonquin. The only doubt he had about his make-up concerned the grey of his hair and eyebrows,

which was provided by talcum powder and could have
been brushed out. His face colouring was a dye and
not a grease paint, and his straggly moustache had been
put on hair by hair with waterproof gum—both of them
were secure against ordinary risks.

Then after a while he knew why he was thinking
along these lines. Because somebody was washing his
face. Or dabbing it with a cold wet cloth. Somebody
was also shaking him by the shoulder and calling a
name that he knew perfectly well.

"Tom! . . . Tom!"

A curiously low voice, for anyone who was trying to
call him. But a voice that he knew, too. And a faint
fragrance in the air that had been in his nostrils before,
some other time when he had heard the voice.

He decided to try opening his eyes, and finally he
made it. But there was no difference. Only blackness
swimming around him. And he knew that his eyes
were open.

He wondered whether he had gone blind.

His head hurt very much, and the shaking at his
shoulder made him dizzy. He wished it would all go
away.

"Tom! Wake up!"

A voice that filled out words like a 'cello; a voice and
a fragrance that would be in his memory always.

"Avalon darling," he murmured sleepily, "I love you
very much, but can't you do anything about your in-
somnia?"

Then everything was utterly still, except for the far
faint lulling whisper of the sea.

It seemed like a good time to go to sleep again.

Then there was a face soft against his cheek, moving;
and a dampness that was not the wet cloth, but warmer;

and the fragrance sweeter and stronger in his senses; and arms and hands clinging and pressing; and the same voice talking and making sounds that merged with the slow soft roll of the sea, and breaking strangely where there were no waves breaking, and speaking and stirring, and this was something that happened a million years ago but had only been waiting a million years to happen, and he had to do something about it even if it meant smashing his way out of an iron vice that was holding him in that absurd and intolerable suspension, and there was the sweetness and the voice saying: "Simon, darling . . . Oh, darling, my darling . . . Simon, wake up, Simon!"

And the voice saying: "I didn't know—I'm such a dope, but I should have . . . Simon, darling wake up! . . . Simon, wake up. . . ."

And then he was awake.

A moment of clarity drifted toward him like a child's balloon, and he caught it and held on to it and everything was quite clear again while he held it.

He said very carefully: "Avalon, I left a message for you that I'd see you to-morrow. Well, this is to-morrow. Only I can't see you. That's silly, isn't it?"

She said: "I had to put the light out again because I didn't want it to show under the door. . . . Simon, dear, wake up! Don't go to sleep again!"

He said: "Why did you come here anyway?"

"Because that creep I was with knew Cookie, and she'd apologised, and she was being as nice as she can be, and I have to work and Hollywood came into the picture, and it seemed like the only graceful thing to do, and I can't fight the whole night club racket, and . . . Simon, you must stay awake!"

"I am awake," he said. "Tell me what happened."

"After Pat hit you, Cookie said that it wasn't your fault that Ferdy went after him—he went by himself, or she sent him, or something. And he was broken-hearted. So we all put you to bed, and everything broke up. Zellermann said that you'd sleep it off——"

"I bet he did. But I never had to sleep off a crack on the jaw before."

"Pat's a strong guy. He carried you upstairs all by himself."

"I've been slugged by strong guys before. Believe it or not. But it never felt like this afterwards. I feel as if I'd been drugged."

"You could have been. You were drinking."

"I was cheat-drinking. I poured the last one myself. But Zellermann could have slipped something into my glass."

"I suppose he could have, in the commotion. . . . Stay awake, Simon. You must!"

"I'm still awake. That's how I know. If I'd had it all, you wouldn't have been able to rouse me now. Hogan stopped that by slugging me. But Zellermann still thought I'd sleep it off. I would have, too, if you hadn't worked on me."

"Simon, are you making sense now?"

"I'm doing everything in the wide world I can." It was still an unforgettable effort to speak concisely and intelligibly. "Give me a chance, baby. I'm working at it. I never was drunk to-night. I sound like it now, but I wasn't."

She was close to him and holding him, her face against his, as if she were trying to transmit her life and wakefulness to him from every inch of her body.

It seemed like a long time; and through all of it he was working through fluctuating waves of awareness to

cling on to the wandering balloon that was his only
actual link with this other world that he had to keep
touch with against all the cruel violation of a dream
and the fumes of a drug that kept creeping back to try
and steal away his will.

She said after a few seconds or a thousand years:
"Darling, you shouldn't have dressed up with that
moustache." He knew that he had to shut out the note
in her voice that hung between a sob and a hysterical
giggle. "It tickles," she said.

"I'm sorry," he said. "Remind me to get rid of it.
Any time when I know what I'm doing."

She roused up beside him.

"Darling, you won't go off again now, will you?"

"No." He rolled over and rolled up. The movement
sent his head whirling away from his body on a weird
trajectory that revolted his stomach. He caught it somehow as it came back, and held it firmly in his hands.
He said meticulously: "Look. You were dabbing my
face with a wet cloth when I came to. You got the wet
cloth from somewhere. Where?"

"There's a bathroom. Here."

Her fingers slid into his hand. He went stumbling
through the dark where she led him, as if his limbs
didn't belong to him any more.

Then he was alone for a while.

A while during which he used every trick and help
that his experience could lend to him. Plus an over-
dose of aspirin from a bottle which he found in a cabinet over the wash-bowl.

Plus an effort of will that tore every nerve in his
body to shreds and put it painstakingly together again.
He never quite knew how he accomplished that. Part
of it came from the native resilience of a perfect phy-

sique in plu-perfect condition, the inestimable reserves of a phenomenal athlete who hadn't been out of training for sixteen years. Part of it came from an unconquerable power of mind that would have torn every cell of its habitation apart and remodelled it to achieve the resuscitation that had to be achieved. The Saint didn't know, and had no sort of inward power to waste on analysing it. He only knew that it took every atom of inward power that he could gouge out of himself, and left him feeling as if he had been drawn through a steam wringer at the end. But he had done what he had set himself to do; and he knew that also.

He didn't even know how long it took; but he knew he had done it when he was finished.

He knew it when he turned out the light in the bathroom and ventured back into the dark to find Avalon, feeling strangely light and vacuous in his bones, but with his mind queerly cool and alive, as if the discipline had purged and polished it to stratopheric limpidity and translucence.

He knew it when she was still waiting for him, and their hands met in the blackness that was not blind any more, and they sat side by side on the edge of a bed, and he could touch the warmth of her hair and say: "It's okay now, Avalon. Honestly. Everything's under control. Now tell me——"

"How did you do it?" she asked, huskily, and close to him, but not leaning on him. "Why were you putting on the act, and what are you doing here?"

"I bought myself a costume and some warpaint," he said lightly, "and here I am, because I was invited. The important thing is—what were you doing, trying to wake me up in the middle of the night?"

"I was afraid," she said, very quietly now.

He could feel the tenseness of her like a strung wire beside him; but he said nothing, keeping her hand steadily in his hand and his shoulder lightly against hers until she went on.

"I told you why I came here."

"I remember."

"I had a scare when I saw Zellermann. Nobody had said anything about him, which they could hardly have helped doing unless they were holding out on purpose. But I didn't want to be silly, so I just tried to pass it off. You heard me. And I thought, Ferdy didn't count at all, and you and Pat were two outside guys who couldn't have been mixed up in anything, and nothing much could happen while you were around. But I was scared, in a silly way, inside. And then, when Pat picked on you for no reason at all, it all came up again."

"I know," said the Saint. "And then?"

"Then I just tried to talk myself out of it, but I didn't get very far with that. But us Dexters never know when to say Uncle. . . . So then I went to bed when everybody else did, when Pat had broken everything up anyway. I thought I could go to sleep and forget it; but I couldn't . . . I just lay awake and listened. . . . And nobody else seemed to go to bed. Nobody tried to open my door, which I'd locked, being a bright girl; but every time I was nearly asleep I could hear people creeping about and muttering. And it never sounded like the sort of noises they'd make if they were just trying to go on with a party. And I went on being afraid all the time. I'm a very imaginative character, don't you think?"

"No," he said. "Not any more than you should be."

"So finally I thought I just had to talk to somebody safe and ordinary again, and I thought you and Pat were the best bet there was. I didn't know what on earth I'd have said to you when I got here, but I'd have thought of something. I always can, being an old hardened expert. . . . But when I crept in here, and had the light on for a moment, and Pat hadn't been to bed at all, and you seemed to be out for keeps as Zellermann said you would be—I suppose I had a moment of panic. So . . . Simon, will you forget me being so stupid? I'm not usually like this. But it's sort of ridiculous, after everything that's gone on, for this to be you."

The Saint seemed to have arms vaguely attached to his body, one of them pressing her against him and the other lying across his lap and becoming conscious of something sharp-edged and metallic in his pocket— something that was definably not small change creased into a fold of his trousers. Something that bothered his forearm and his thigh pocket, so that he put his hand into his trouser pocket to fumble and identify it, while he was talking. . . . He still had to cling on to every item of his hard-won clarity, inch upon inch.

He said: "Avalon, I've got to tell you two or three things as sharply as I can make it. I'll fill in the details later, when we have time. If we have time. But probably you can do that for yourself anyway."

She said: "Yes, darling."

"If you can't, you'll have to take my word for it. We're right in the middle of a situation where human life is cheaper than the air. I'm going to try to make sense, and I want you to listen closely. I'm sure I can't do it twice."

"I won't interrupt," she said.

The Saint fastened his mind on what he wanted to say. He forced himself with tremendous effort to expand the phrase "Benny sent me" into a broad picture.

"The relationship between 903 Bubbling Well Road in Shanghai and Dean's Dock and Warehouse Company in Brooklyn is not apparent on any map. But it's there. I know it. I came along on this clambake to snap the cord that ties those two locations together. This joint is where one end of it is anchored. You've got to see the theory before you can understand the problem."

He rested for a moment. It was still harder than he would have believed to marshal his thoughts.

"Once there was a man who got an idea. For the sake of convenience let's call him Dr. Ernst Zellermann, though it may be somebody else. His idea was utterly simple: If you can supply a man with narcotics you can make him into a tool. The war shot the dope-smuggling racket into its proper hell, but revival on a large scale was forecast when Hiroshima became a subject for history books. And that's where 903 Bubbling Well Road entered the picture."

He paused again.

"Let's assume that some person or persons glaumed on to the bulk of available opium in the Orient. Collaborationists, almost certainly. They established a headquarters, stored their supplies, and awaited the inevitable ending of hostilities. They knew that merchant ships would soon be coming, and that many of these ships would have touched at New York. So Dr. Z. collects a pal or two and sets up a place here. For the sake of clarity let's call it Cookie's Canteen. Merchant seamen are invited, everything free, even a roll of hay with whatever hostess a boy can promote. Our likely character is wined and dined at Cookie's Cellar, everything still on the house. If he exhibits certain desirable larcenous tendencies—which would be revealed under

questioning by a clever psychiatrist—the pitch is made.
And the Mad Hatter said plaintively: 'It was the best
butter'——"

Avalon said: "Huh?"

The Saint took another grip on himself, brought his
conscious mind up from whirling in dark chasms, lifted
it with every ounce of will power he could command.

"Sorry, I wandered. . . . The pitch was made. 'How
would you like to make some extra money, chum, and
here's a hundred on account? Just go to 903 Bubbling
Well Road and say Benny sent you. Bring back the
packages you'll be given, bring them here, and collect
some more money.' . . . So our lad does it. Now the sale
and distribution of the dope won't bring in enough to
pay the overhead of a really big-scale set-up like this,
so Operation B goes into effect. A doctor can supply
patients with narcotics, can turn them into hopheads
more safely than anybody else. Then, by shutting off
the supply, he can get almost anything in return for
more dope to ease the craving. Blackmail—or services.
That's where Dean's Warehouse and Docking Company
is tied up with Operation A, or Shanghai. The hopheads
knock it over, bring in the sheaves—of furs, jewels,
whisky, whatnot. Or a bank is held up, instead. Or anything. A whole empire of crime begins to spread out
from one central system."

The Saint sighed. He was weary. Avalon took his
hand in hers.

"So that's it," she said. "That explains a lot of things
I didn't understand before. Why they'd go overboard
for some creep who knew the difference between port
and starboard and nothing else."

They were still keeping their voices very low, as if
they were in a room full of ears.

"This is all new to you?" Simon asked expressionlessly.

"Why do you ask that?"

"I thought I would. I've told you all this because it doesn't matter now how much anybody knows I know."

The Saint's fingers had almost finished with the odd metal shape in his pocket. And the message which had begun to spell itself slothfully out from it by some multi-dimensional alchemy between his finger-tips and his remembrance began to sear his brain with a lambent reality that cauterised the last limp tissues of vagueness out of his awakening.

He felt his own grip biting into her flesh.

"Avalon," he said, in a voice that came from a long way off in the dark. "You've been in this up to the neck from the beginning. You might even have started a lot of it—for all of us—by that parting crack of yours about the Saint after I socked Zellermann. But the play-acting is over, and I must know something now."

"What, darling?" she asked; and her voice was so easy in contrast to his own that he knew where he had to keep his own sanities together.

"I must know which side you're on, Avalon. Even if you haven't had any sense—even if it's all words of one syllable now. Are you going all the way with me, or is this just an excursion?"

It seemed as if she stiffened beside him for an instant, and then softened so that she was closer and more real than ever before.

Her voice came from a great distance also in the darkness between them.

"You damn fool," she said. "I worship the ground you walk on. I want you more than I ever wanted anyone in my whole life, or ever will."

They were both very quiet then, as if something had been said which should never have been put into words.

And there were other sounds far away, faint frettings against the monotonous rolling of the sea.

The Saint's fingers touched the hard sharp metal in his trouser pocket for one last assurance, and brought it out. He said very matter-of-factly: "Can you find a match, Avalon?"

She was in movement all around him, and he kept still; and then there was a sudden hurtful flare of light that flickered agonisingly over the scrap of embossed metal that he had taken out of his pocket and held toward her in the palm of his hand.

"No," he said, without any inflexion. "Not mine. Pat Hogan must have stuck his badge into my pocket as a last desperate resort—as a clue or a signal of some kind. He never knew me from Adam. But he was an under-cover man in this racket for the Treasury Department."

2

The match flickered once more and went out, leaving him with the moulding of her face stamped on his memory. And he knew that that was not only printed by one match, but by more lights than he had seen in many years.

"How long have you known that?" she asked.

"Only since I found the badge and figured it out," he said. "But that's long enough. . . . Until then, I'm afraid I was off with some very wrong ideas. When I picked him up at the Canteen this evening I happened to see that he was going heeled—he had a gun in his hip pocket—and I began wondering. I've been listening to his rather shaky brogue all night, and watching him sell the blarney to Kay Natello, who never could be a sailor's swateheart no matter what else; and I knew before we left town that there was something screwy in the set-up. . . . But I had everything else wrong. I had Hogan figured as one of the Ungodly, and I thought he was playing his game against me."

"If he wasn't," she said, "why did he pick on you and knock you out?"

"To get me out of the way. He didn't know who I was. I was playing the part of a blabber-mouthed drunken sailor, and just doing it too damn well. I was doing everything I could to make myself interesting to Cookie and Zellermann anyhow. I was barging around in the dark, and I happened to hit a nail on the head by mentioning Shanghai. So I was something to work on. And I was being worked on, the last thing I remember. But Hogan didn't want me being propositioned. His job was to get the goods on this gang, so he wanted to be propositioned himself. I might have been too drunk to remember, or I might have refused to testify. So he had to create a good interruption and break it up. And he did a lovely job, considering the spot he was in."

"I'm getting some of my faith back," she said. "If a government man knocks you cold, that's legitimate; but you can't let anybody else do it. Not if I'm going to love you."

He smiled very fractionally in the gloom, and his hand lay on her wrist in a touch that was not quite a caress, but something to which nothing had to be added and from which nothing could be taken away.

"And now," he said, "I suppose you're wondering where I belong in this, and why Hogan doesn't know me."

"I didn't ask you."

"I might as well tell you. Hogan is doing his best, and so is the Department over him; but this thing goes too far over the world, into too many countries and too many jurisdictions. Only an organisation that's just as international can cope with it. There is such a thing, and I'm part of it. That's all I'm allowed to say."

"And meanwhile," she said, with a coldness that was not really her, "why isn't Pat in bed? And why did he leave you his badge?"

"Either because he's still trying to wring the last drop out of his act, or because he's trying to do some more dangerous snooping. Either because he hoped he could tip me off to keep my mouth shut and give him a chance, or because he knew he was facing the high jump and if he made a bad landing he hoped I might get some word out for him." The Saint stood up. "Either way, I'm going to find out."

He heard and felt the rustle of her quick movement out of his sight; and then she was in front of him, face to face, and her arms around him and his hand under the soft eaves of her hair.

"Simon—are you all right now?"

"I'm as much use as I'll ever be to-night." His smile was still invisible through the darkness, and in some ways he was glad of it. His touch was strong and tender together. He said: "And Pat did his best, and I'm sure nothing is going to wait for him."

He kissed her again and held her against him; and he remembered a great many things, perhaps too many, and perhaps too many of them were not with her. But none of that mattered any more.

He let her go presently, and in time it had only been a moment.

"I suppose," he said, "you wouldn't happen to have

any artillery in your week-end kit? A machine-gun
might be useful; but if you're travelling light a small
stiletto would help."

"I haven't anything better than a pair of nail
scissors."

"I'm afraid," Simon said sadly, "it might be hard
to persuade Zellermann to sit still for that."

Light slashed through the room like a stealthy blade
as he found the door handle and opened it.

The corridor outside was dim and lifeless; but as he
stepped out into it the sea murmurs were left in the
room behind him, and the other stirrings of sound that
had crept through to him in there resolved themselves
into their own individual pattern—a rumble and twitter
of muffled voices and movement downstairs. There was
no movement that could be identified and no single
word that could be picked out; but they had a pitch
and a rhythm of deadly deliberation that spilled
feathery icicles along his spine. He knew very well now
why Avalon hadn't been able to sleep, and why she
had come looking for Pat Hogan or Tom Simons or
anyone else solid and ordinary and potentially safe
and wholesome. As she had said, they weren't the sort
of noises that people made if they were just trying to
go on with a party. You couldn't put a finger on any
one solitary thing about them; but if you had a certain
kind of sensitivity, you knew. . . . There was a quality
of evil and terror that could set a pace and a key even
in confused and distant mutterings.

It made the Saint feel strangely naked and ineffectual as he moved toward it, with the whirling but no
longer dizzy hollowness left in his head by the drug,
and the unaccustomed formality of his muscular co-
ordinations, and the cold knowledge that he had

nothing to fight with but his own uncertain strength and uprooted wits. But Patrick Hogan—or whatever his real name was—had exposed himself in just as lonely a way for the job that he had to do; and his gun couldn't have helped him much, or the sounds below would have been different. And other men on more obvious battle-fronts had done what they could with what they had, because wars didn't wait.

He didn't feel particularly glorious or heroic about it: it was much more a coldly predestined task that had to be finished. It didn't seem to spread any emotion on the fact that it could easily and probably be his own finish too. It was just an automatic and irresistible mechanism of placing one foot in front of another on a necessary path from which there was no turning back, although the mind could sit away and watch its own housing walking voluntarily toward oblivion.

And this was it, and he was it, for one trivial tremendous moment, himself, personally—the corny outlaw who redeemed himself in the last reel.

It was quite funny, and a lot of fun, in the way he was thinking.

He was moving like a cat, his ears travelling far ahead of his feet, and a new sound began to intrude upon them. A sound of voices. One voice detached itself from the two that were in converse, and a bell rang inside the Saint's head with brazen clangour.

It was the voice that had called Dr. Zellermann on the night the Saint had broken into the office.

And it was the voice of Ferdinand Pairfield.

Lightly and quickly, Simon pulled Avalon toward the closed door through which seeped the words of Dr. Zellermann and the fair Ferdinand.

"I won't do it," Ferdinand said. "That is your job,

and you must complete it. You really must, Ernst."

The Saint was shocked. This voice wasn't fluttery, seeming always ready to trail off into a graceful gesture. This voice was venomous, reminding one of a beautiful little coral snake, looking like a pretty bracelet, coiled to strike and inject the poison that is more deadly, drop for drop, than that of the King Cobra. Here was no witless fag with a penchant for *Crème Violette*; here was a creature who could command in terms of death.

The Saint's brain gave one last dizzy lurch, and then settled into a clear thin stratospheric stillness as the last disjointed fragments of the picture he had been working for fell into mesh. In some strange way that one incongruous touch had reconciled all other incongruities—the freakish fellowship of Dr. Zellermann with Cookie and Kay Natello, of all of them with Sam Jeffries and Joe Hyman, even the association with the lobster-eyed James Prather and the uninhibited Mrs. Gerald Meldon. His own mistake had been in accepting as merely another piece of the formula the one ingredient which was actually the catalyst for them all. It was a weird and yet strangely soothing sensation to realise at last, with the utter certainty of psychic confirmation, that the man he had been looking for, the anchor thread of the whole fantastic web, was Mr. Ferdinand Pairfield.

3

Simon became aware of Avalon's fingers cramping on his arm, and knew that her perceptions were stumbling after his, less surely for one thing because she still lacked so much background that he had not been able to sketch for her, but following him more in mad surmise than with the integrated sureness that directed him.

He pressed his hand over hers and went on listening, as Pairfield said: "It'd be dreadful to lose you, but of course you know how much the F.B.I. would like to know the truth about why you became a refugee from Vienna. I've taken care of you all this time, but I can't go on doing it for ever. If you let me down and any-thing happens——"

"I don't want to let you down, Ferdinand," Zeller-mann said; and through all the measured confidence of his accents Simon had a vision of the smooth brow shining like damp ivory. "But our methods are getting nowhere. I think he'll die before he tells us what he knows."

"He'd better not," Ferdinand said in the same deadly bell-like voice. "I want all the information he has. And I shall not assist you. You know the sight of torture and pain sickens me. I should simply die."

"You didn't seem particularly affected in the case of Foley."

"Oh, but I was! When I stuck that knife in him, I almost fainted. It was thrilling! But that's another case in point. It should have been unnecessary for me to do it. You knew that he was toying with the idea of selling us out, and blackmailing us to boot. You should have handled it."

The Saint could almost see Zellermann shrug.

"You won't come and help us?"

"I simply couldn't. Get down there again. I want that information immediately."

Simon pulled Avalon away from the door, and they fled on cat feet down the corridor and stood very still pressed against the wall. Dr. Zellermann came out of

Ferdinand's room and went downstairs without a glance in their direction.

Now the Saint had purpose. Each task in its turn, and the silencing of the golden boy was first. He strode to the door and flung it open. Ferdinand, clad in a pale cerise dressing-gown, turned and saw the Saint.

He looked up casually and a little irritably, as if he only expected to see Zellermann coming back with an afterthought excuse. When he saw the Saint, his expression remained outwardly unchanged. His reaction came from deep under his skin, instead of being the muscular contortion of a moment's shock. It came out as a dew of sweat on his face that swelled into an established wetness; and only after that was established his pretty face went pinched and pallid with terror. He didn't have to say anything to make a complete confession that he was answering his own questions as fast as they could spiral through his reeling mind, and that he knew that the answers were all his own and there was nothing he could say to anyone else, anywhere. He wasn't the first dilettante in history who had been caught up with by the raw facts of life in the midst of all the daffodils and dancing, and he would not be the last.

The Saint felt almost sorry for him; but all the pity in the world didn't alter the absolute knowledge that Mr. Pairfield constituted a very real menace to the peace and quiet which Simon wanted for a few seconds more. Mr. Pairfield's eyes inflated themselves like a pair of small blowfish at what they divined; his mouth dropped open, and his throat tightened in the preliminary formation of a scream. These were only the immediate reflex responses blossoming out of the trough of terror that was already there, but they were no less urgent and dangerous for that. Something had to be done about them, and there was really only one thing to do.

Simon put out his left hand and grasped the lapels of Mr. Pairfield's dainty silk dressing-gown together, and drew him closer with a sympathetic smile.

"Ferdy," he said, "don't you know that it's time for all good little girls to be asleep?"

And with that his right fist rocketed up to impinge on Mr. Pairfield's æsthetic chin, and sleep duly followed.

Simon slid an arm under him as he crumpled, and carried him back into the room and dumped him on the bed. It was a nice encouraging thing to discover and prove that he still had that much strength and vitality in him, even though he knew very well that the power and agility that were required to anæsthetise Ferdinand Pairfield would not necessarily be enough to cope with anyone who was at least averagely tough of mind and body. It made him feel a new sureness of himself and a new hope that slipped looseningly and warmingly into his limbs as he tore one of Cookie's fine percale sheets into wide ribbons to tie Ferdinand's wrists and ankles to the bed, and then to stuff into his slackly open mouth and gag him.

He found himself working with the swift efficiency of second nature; and that was a good feeling too, to be aware of the old deftness and certainty flowing into his own movements with increasing ease all the time, and the gossamer bubble of his wakefulness holding and not breaking but growing more clear and durable with each passing minute.

He finished, and then made a quick search of the room and the person of his test specimen, looking for one thing only; but it seemed that Mr. Pairfield's wanderings into wickedness hadn't taken the course of acquiring any of the useful armaments of evil. No doubt he was glad to delegate all such crudities to underlings. The Saint ended his brief quest still weaponless; yet he gave it up with a glance at Avalon that had all the care-free lights of supreme laughter in its blue brilliance.

"Knock 'em off one by one," he remarked—"as the bishop said as he surveyed the new line-up of thespian talent of the Follies. That's our motto. Shall we move on to the next experiment?"

Their hands touched momentarily, and then he was out of the room and on his way down the stairs.

On his way, with the new chill, ugly knowledge that the palpitating fright of Ferdinand Pairfield could only have been germinated by something that had been there in that house before any board creaked and Pairfield had thrown his door open and seen the Saint. And that that something, whatever form it took, could only be deadly for the Federal man who had called himself Patrick Hogan—if it hadn't been conclusively deadly already.

Or if simple death might not be much better than what could be going on.

Simon was at the foot of the stairs, in the hall, with the front door only a few steps away; and Avalon was still close beside him. Escape would have been easy for them. But he knew without even wordless asking that neither of them had thought of that. Her eyes were steady and quiet and only inquiring as they met his again. The sounds that came through the solid closed door of the living-room were strangely distorted and dreadful in their muffled distortion.

The Saint saw her throat move as she listened and looked at him; but her gaze was only waiting, always.

Their hands met and held that time, for an instant;

and something quirked over his lips that could have been a smile, but wasn't. Then he left her.

He didn't go to the living-room door, but vanished the other way, toward the kitchen.

In a few seconds more he was back, and he brought with him a stag-handled carving knife. The blade was strong and gleaming, and he tested it with his thumb before he slid it up his left sleeve and held it there with the pressure of a bent elbow against the flat of the blade.

His lips almost touched her ear, and he spoke in a voice that was only the echo of a whisper.

"Get on your horse, darling," he said. "Sneak out of here and grab one of the cars outside while I keep 'em busy. Drive into town and recruit some large healthy cops. Bring 'em back just as fast as you can. And have breakfast with me."

She only shook her head. Her long hair brushed his mouth.

He couldn't argue with her there.

He left her and hoped that she would go, and knew that she wouldn't. He was glad and yet bitter about that; but it was a confusion of things that he could only take as they broke over him and save to be struggled with some other time.

He had to end this other thing first, no matter how.

He went to the door that the sounds came through, and stooped to put an eye to the keyhole for a second's preview of what he had to walk into. And it was curious that while his face turned to stone his only detached mental reaction was that it was merely exactly what he had imagined in a distant nightmare of unbearable understanding. He had that unreal sensation of being a long way off from all of it, away somewhere, even while the nerve endings curdled under his skin and he began to move under an impetus that was altogether instinctive and altogether quixotic and absurd.

Even while he heard the air-conditioned voice of Dr. Ernst Zellermann, cool and persuasive like the voice of a society psycho-analyst in a darkened consulting-room, the only distinct articulate sound that he caught and held afterwards, saying: "Why not be reasonable, Patrick, and get it into your head that I must go on until you tell me exactly how much you've been able to accomplish with your masquerade?"

The keyhole glimpse wiped out into a full picture as Simon opened the door.

It was something that would haunt him all his life, something that belonged in a Grand Guignol school of outlandish horror, that was so much worse because the mind had heard all about it long ago, and long ago dismissed it as a ghoulish fantasy. Now it was real after all, and the reality had a chill intellectual impact that was capable of leaving scars on the memory of even such a man as the Saint, who thought he had already seen most variations of what there was to be seen in the pathology of macabre dreadfulness.

The figure of Dr. Zellermann, standing poised and cool with his smooth silver locks and fine ascetic profile and a long cigarette clipped in his sensitive fingers and treasuring half an inch of unshaken ash, was a stock item in its way. So was the figure of Patrick Hogan, bound hand and foot in a chair, with the sweat of agony running down into his eyes and the lower half of his face covered with the gag through which some of those horrible formless strangled sounds had come. It was the two women squatting beside him—Cookie with her crude bloated face no longer wearing its artificial smile, and Natello with the sallow skin stretched tight over the bones of her skull and her haggard eyes smouldering with a light of weird absorption. The women, and what they were doing. . . .

And this was the reality of half-remembered legend-histories of Messalina, of tales of the Tuareg women commissioned to the ritual torture of their captives, of witches out of a dim universal folk-lore bent to the consummation of some black sacrament of pain. This was what gave a sudden dimension and articulation to his ambiguous impressions of Cookie and Natello, just as in their separate ways the performance seemed to breathe blood and life into them, hardening and en-rooting the slobbish grossness of Cookie and illuminating Natello's starved ethereal gawkiness—even throwing a pale reflection of its hot heathen glow on Zellermann's satanically connoisseurish frigidity. This, that some-how crystallised and focused all the twisted negations and perversions that were inherent in the philosophy they served. This new scientific and persuasive bar-barism, aptly and symbolically framed in the gleam-ing chrome-plated jungle of a Pairfield-decorated par-lour. . . .

But for Simon Templar it was a symbol too; and more than that it was a trial and evidence and verdict, and a sentence that only waited for an execution that would be a pride and a clean pleasure to remember with the ugliness that began it.

He walked into the room empty-handed, with the carving knife in his sleeve held by the pressure of his bent left arm.

Zellermann held his cigarette with the ash unbroken in his left hand, and his right hand dropped into the side pocket of his beautifully tailored coat. Aside from the lightning switch of his bleached grey eyes, that was his only movement. But it was quite adequate for what it meant.

The Saint didn't even seem to notice it.

He was Tom Simons again, perfectly and entirely, for the few steps that he had to take. They seemed to stretch out for an infinity of distance and an eternity of time; but no one who watched him could have seen how every cell and fibre of him was wrung out in the achievement of that convincing unconsciousness of their importance. He lurched quite clumsily in his walk, and his stare trying to hold Zellermann was blank and glazed—and those were the easiest tricks in his act.

"'Ullo, Doc," he mouthed. "Wot abaht one fer the road?"

He was in a dream where every second seemed to take a week to crawl by, and you could stop overnight to analyse every inching flicker of event.

He saw Zellermann relax fractionally, even embark on the mental prologue to an elaborate clinical evaluation of drug reactions. He saw Cookie and Kay Natello rising and turning toward him with a mixture of uncertainty and fear and hope. He saw everything, without looking directly at any of it.

"You must be made out of iron, Tom," Zellermann said admiringly, and as if he had learned the formula from a book. "You just about put us all under the table. We were going to bed."

The Saint staggered closer to him.

"I bin to bed once," he said. "But I'm thirsty. Honester-gawd. Coudden I 'ave just one more drop before closing time?"

Then his wandering gaze seemed to catch sight of Hogan for the first time.

"Swelp me," he said, "that's 'im! The —— 'oo 'it me! All tied up shipshape so 'e 'as ter be'yve. Just lemme 'ave one crack at 'im——"

"Patrick just had too much to drink," Zellermann said. "We're trying to get him to bed . . ."

He actually moved closer, suavely and with almost contemptuous skill, interposing himself between Simon and the uglier details of his specialised treatment for intoxication.

The Saint blinked at him blearily, swaying another step and two steps nearer.

It looked fine and perfect until the doctor's glance suddenly switched and hardened on a point beyond the Saint's shoulder, and the whole calm patronising balance of his body hardened with it as if it had been nipped in an interstellar frost.

And even then, only one precise unit of him moved— the hand that still rested in his coat pocket. But that movement was still as adequate and eloquent as it had been the first time.

Simon didn't need any manuals or blueprints to work it out. He knew, with that endless impersonality of comprehension, that Avalon Dexter had started to follow him into the room, and that Zellermann had seen her, and that the shining wheels that ran in Zellermann's brain had spun an instantaneous web together, and that rightly or wrongly the web had enough tensile strength in Zellermann's mind for Zellermann to work on it.

The Saint's own movement actually followed and resulted from Zellermann's; and yet it was like the clicking of a switch and the awakening of a light, so that it was almost simultaneous.

He heard the splitting blast of Zellermann's gun in

the same quantum as he was aware of stumbling sideways and straightening his left arm so that the bone handle of the carving knife dropped into the curved fingers of his waiting left hand, and then he was aware of a searing pang in his left arm and a shocking blow that spun him half around, but he had his balance again in the same transposition, and his right hand took the haft of the knife as it dropped and drew it clear of the sleeve and turned it and drove it straight with the same continued gesture into Zellermann's chest, just a little to one side of the breastbone and a hand's breadth below the carnation in his button hole.

Then he left the knife there where it stuck and took Zellermann's automatic away as the doctor's fingers loosened on it, ripping it clear of the pocket at about the moment when Zellermann's shoulders rolled on the floor, and fired again and again while he was still rising and Cookie was starting toward him with her broad muscular hands reaching out and Natello was still swinging back the hot curling-iron that she had been playing with.

They were the first women that Simon Templar had ever killed, and he did it rather carefully and conscientiously, in the pellucid knowledge of what they were and what they had done, and to his own absolute judicial satisfaction, shooting Kay Natello three inches above her hollow navel and Cookie in the same umbilical bull's-eye, as closely as he could estimate it through her adipose camouflage.

4

Hamilton said almost plaintively: "Couldn't you arrange to leave more than one prisoner, just once in a while?"

"Could you arrange to have people stop attacking me?" asked the Saint. "Self-defence is so tempting. Besides, think how much I save the country on trials and attorneys. I ought to get a rebate on my income tax for it."

"I'll speak to the President about it right away."

"Anyway, I left you the kingpin—and I think he's got the kind of imagination that'll do some real suffering while he's waiting for his turn in the death house. I feel rather happy about that—which is why I left him."

"Before your tender heart gets you into any more trouble," Hamilton said, "you'd better get out of there if you can. I'll talk to you again in New York. I've got another job for you."

"You always have," said the Saint. "I'll get out. Hogan can hold the fort long enough."

He cradled the telephone and looked at the Federal man again. He said: "It's all yours, Patrick. Washington wants me out of the limelight. As usual. . . . By the way, is the name really Hogan?"

The other nodded. Simon had done all that he could for him: he would be able to hold the fort. And other forts again. His face was still pale and drawn and shiny, but there was no uncertainty in it. It was a good face, moulded on real foundations, and durable.

"Sure," he said. "Hogan's the name. But I was born in New Jersey, and I have to work like hell on the brogue." He was studying the Saint while he talked, quite frankly and openly, but with a quiet respect that was a natural part of his reversion from the character part he had been playing, sitting very laxly but squarely in an arm-chair with the glass of brandy that Simon had poured for him, conserving and gathering his strength. He said: "You had me fooled. Your Cockney's a lot better. And that make-up—it is a make-up, isn't it?"

"I hope so," said the Saint with a smile. "I'd hate to look like this for the rest of my life."

"I didn't expect anything like this when I left my badge in your pocket. I was just clutching at a straw. I figured it was a thousand to one it wouldn't do me any good. I thought you were just another drunken sailor—in fact, I let you pick me up just for that, so I could watch what this gang would do with you."

The Saint laughed a little.

Avalon Dexter finished binding up his arm with torn strips of another of Cookie's expensive sheets. She was very cool and efficient about it. He moved his arm and tested the bandage approvingly; then he began to wriggle into his jacket again. Zellermann's one shot had missed the bone: the bullet had passed clean through, and the flesh wound would take care of itself.

He said: "Thanks, darling."

She helped him with his coat.

He said: "Go on quoting me as just another drunken sailor, Pat. You don't even have to bring me into this finale. The witnesses won't talk. So Tom Simons woke up, and was drunk and sore and scared, and scrammed the hell out. He went back to his ship, and nobody cares about him, anyway. Let him go. Because I am going anyway, while you take the 'phone and start calling to your squads to take care of the bodies."

"What about Miss Dexter?" Hogan asked practically.

"She was scared too, and she scrammed independently. You know about her and how they were trying to use her. Leave her out of it if you can; but if you need her we've got her address in New York. I'll steal one of the cars and take her back with me. Hamilton will okay it. The police in New York were warned long ago, it seems—when Zellermann tried to frame me at 21, they went through a performance to make Zellermann think he'd gotten me out of the way, but they turned me loose at once."

"Okay, Saint. When you call that Imperative exchange in Washington, I say Uncle anyhow. But I can look after this. And—thank you."

They shook hands around. Hogan stayed seated in his chair. He could keep going. He was still full of questions, but he was too well trained to ask them.

"Let's get together one day," said the Saint, and meant it just like that.

He went out with Avalon.

They talked very ordinarily and quietly on the drive back, as if they had known each other for a long while, which they had, while the dawn lightened slowly around them and drew out the cool sweetness of the dew on the peaceful fields. The red-gold casque of her hair was pillowed on his shoulder as they slipped into the rousing murmur of Manhattan in the bright sunlight of another day.

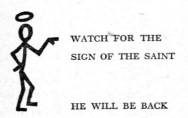

WATCH FOR THE

SIGN OF THE SAINT

HE WILL BE BACK